MW01644366

NOTE: This is a work of fiction. Names, characters, places, and incidents are a product of the author's imagination. Any resemblance to real life is purely coincidental. All characters in this story are 18 or older.

Liam & Lizzie

Willow Winters &
Lauren Landish
Wall Street Journal & USA Today Bestselling Authors

From USA Today bestselling authors, Willow Winters and Lauren Landish, comes a sizzling and tempting romance about the bad boy you can't resist.

I lived my life with no regrets.
Until she showed up.

It started with her old man. That stubborn bastard set me up. He knew what he was doing, and I fell for his daughter before I even heard her voice.

What was he thinking,
trying to set her up with a prick like me?

She's too good for me.
I should've walked away,
but every time she told me no,
it only made me want to chase her more.

I shouldn't have brought her into my life.
I'm trouble, that's all I am,
and I brought that to her doorstep.

But I can't let her go now, even if she hates me for it.
She tempted me; now she's mine.

Tempted

Prologue

Liam

That old man knew exactly what he was doing. He fucking set me up. All those times he talked about his sunshine, Elizabeth. All those pictures he showed me? Not to mention all the stories he'd tell me when I was keeping him company. Of course I fell for her before I even heard her voice.

And now I'm fucked. *She's* fucked. What was he thinking, trying to set her up with a no-good asshole like me? She's too fucking good for me. He had to know it.

I'm trouble, that's all I am, and I brought that to her doorstep.

Those gorgeous blue eyes stare back at me with something deeper in them than lust. I've finally won her over. Every bit of her.

I'm a fucking prick for doing it. I know I should've let her down easy. I should've walked away and turned my back on her. Shit, I should've never chased her.

She's a smart girl; she knows I'm no good for her. And it's true. I've got a death threat in my back pocket in the form of her picture, and it's all because of me.

What was her father doing pulling this shit? He knew the hard truth about me. I shake my head, hating how I'm blaming him. The old man's dead now. I'm such a piece of shit, trying to put this all on him and throw the blame on someone other than me.

I pushed her to cave to me. I just needed a taste. And now that I've got her and a good fucking reason to leave this life behind, it's all crashing down around me. But she's here now, and she's in danger.

"Whatever you're thinking, Liam, you need to stop it," she says, and her soft, sweet voice is so damn soothing. Her small hand cups my cheek and I quickly nip her thumb playfully. She lets out a cute squeal, and her eyes quickly heat with desire. I try to give her a small smile, but I can't force it.

She bites down on her bottom lip and softly says, "You worry too much." She looks up at me through her thick lashes. I can't deny her. I'm addicted to her touch.

I take her curvy body in my arms, feeling her soft, lush

frame melt into me. "Only when it involves you," I respond with more honesty than she'll ever know.

She gives me a sweet smile and nudges her nose against mine with her eyes closed. She wants me to take her right now. And I can't deny her that wish. I take her lips with my own, and press my tongue against the seam of her full lips, as she yields to my touch with a kiss. She parts easily for me, spreading her legs and straddling me. She gives in so easily now.

She's learned to trust me.

She's learned to love me and everything I do to her. *If only she knew.*

"You don't have to worry," she says, and she's nearly panting now, her voice trembling with need. "Just take care of me."

I know what she means by that.

Fuck, it's like a bullet to my heart how much she trusts me. I run my hand down my face and stare into her eyes. Her forehead is slightly pinched, and her mouth is parted. Her haze of desire is starting to be replaced with a look of confusion. She doesn't know why I'm hesitating.

I have to tell her. She's going to fucking hate me. She's going to know she was right about me all along.

I nip her bottom lip, and my dick twitches as she closes her eyes and moans. Her hands tangle in my hair and I decide right then--I'm not going to let her go. Even if she hates me. I can't risk it; I can't risk *her.*

One more night with her. Just one more night between us. And then I'll tell her. She's going to fucking hate me. But she's not leaving. I can't let her.

They know she's gotten to me. I can't leave her now, it's too late.

She tempted me; now she's mine.

Chapter 1

Lizzie

The somber chime of church bells greets me as I step out of my car, a red 2015 Toyota Camry. My legs feel shaky as my shoes touch the ground, and for a moment, I'm hit by a surge of weakness as I lean against the car for support.

I can't do this.

But I have to.

For daddy.

Every moment is a struggle, but I manage to stand up straight and close my car door. I take a moment to gather myself, breathing in deeply and fighting back tears before looking up into the dark clouds above.

Why did you take him from me? I demand angrily. *What*

did I do to deserve this? As if in response, there's a deep rumble in the distance, a dark foreboding sound that threatens to take even more from me. But I have nothing left. I feel numb and hollow.

A loud crack splits the sky. He didn't deserve to die! My stepfather was a good man. It's not fair.

Bitterly, I tear my eyes away from the unforgiving heavens and begin making my way through the parking lot. A cool breeze sweeps the area, causing the hem of my black dress to lift up around my thighs and goosebumps to rise on my flesh. Numbly, I ignore it and continue on.

Ahead, I see people walking up the church steps and anxiety tightens around my heart. There are a lot of familiar faces, a few faces I'd rather not speak to, and some I don't know. Even from this distance I can already see the pity in their eyes and hear their empty condolences. It angers me. A lot of them couldn't give a fuck about my father. Or me. They're just here to see me break down.

I vow to put on a strong front, not let them see me cry.

They're all frauds, I think disdainfully. *Half of these people disliked my dad when he was alive, and now they want to pretend like they care.*

It irks me, makes me angry. And I cling to that anger to keep me from being consumed with grief. I'm certain some of these people weren't invited to the funeral, and yet here they are anyway.

As I make it to the church steps, a familiar voice pierces my awareness. "Lizzie?"

I spin around, my dress swirling around my legs, and see my childhood friend, Natalie Doubet, standing there with a large, silver tray of cookies in her hands. Garbed in a black lace dress, her dark blonde hair is pulled up into a severe bun and she's opted for subdued, conservative makeup.

I'm awash with relief. Of all the people I recognize filing into the church, Natalie is the only one I'm happy to lay eyes on.

"Nat!" I cry. I wish my lips would turn up into a smile, but they refuse.

"Hey Lizzie," she says, and her voice is soft, soothing. I just want to melt in her arms.

I run up to her, my arms outstretched.

"Whoa!" Natalie snaps, twisting her body to protect her delicious cargo. "Watch the cookies!"

Despite feeling like shit, I laugh and gently reach out to stroke her arm. Good ol' Nat and her testy temper. "Sorry."

"Don't be. I didn't mean to snap at you, I just didn't want you to get sugar cookies all over your dress." Natalie nods at the church. I can see the sadness in Natalie's eyes as she looks at me, and I fight back the tears that threaten to stream down my face like a waterfall.

"Let's go find the reception so I can put these down and I'll walk with you."

"Okay," I manage.

As we make our way into the church, I'm greeted by distant relatives and past acquaintances. I do my best to hold it together, fighting back tears as each person hugs me and offers their condolences. It's impossibly hard, especially enduring the comments of the more fake and phony guests, and several times I almost start wailing with grief. Somehow, I survive the group without breaking down and then Nat and I head farther into the church.

In the reception room there's already a small crowd milling about, chatting in hushed tones. I lock eyes with more faces I haven't seen in years, and then look away. I know it's only a matter of time before I'm surrounded and barraged with false sympathy again. I'm dreading every second of it.

"I'm so sorry for your loss," Natalie says as soon as she sets the tray of cookies down on the refreshments table. She gives me a big, warm embrace, and once again, I'm fighting back tears. Will it ever end? "I knew Turner was getting up there in age," she remarks, pulling away, "but he looked fine every time I saw him come into the bakery."

It's a struggle to even speak. "He was here one day, and then gone the next," I croak.

Natalie shakes her head solemnly. "I know, right? It's crazy."

A tear escapes my right eye and trails down my cheek. "I don't understand," I moan, angrily wiping away the offending tear with the back of my hand. "I thought cancer took time. I thought there were signs." It hurts. It hurts so much to think there was nothing I could have done to save him. If only I could go back in time.

Nat clamps a hand on my shoulder, her eyes clouded with sympathy. "I don't know what to say, Liz, except... sometimes these things happen."

But why did it have to happen to him? I want to scream out. *It's not fair!*

"If you need anything while you're in town, I don't care what it is," Nat continues, pulling me into another warm embrace, "I'm here for you."

"Thank you," I say simply, swallowing the huge lump in my throat.

After rubbing my back for a few moments, Natalie pulls away and peers at me. "You look good at least, like you lost a lot of weight." She pauses and then adds, "I'm so sorry, I didn't mean to come off like that."

I brush away her worry. "You're fine. I wasn't eating much before the news, and I ate even less after I heard it. Stress, you know?" I had just finished with finals when I got the news. I have a little over two months before my last semester. Until then, I'm here. Back in my hometown, mourning the death of the only family I ever had.

Natalie gestures at her tray of goodies. "You should try one of my sugar cookies. I guarantee they'll get you back on track." She gestures to her stomach and adds, "They're a bit fattening."

I snicker at her little joke and roll my eyes. "You're beautiful."

She giggles and straightens the tray with a small smile.

I glance at her baked morsels. While I'm not hungry, they do look delicious. Each cookie is a rich golden color, iced and dusted with multicolored powder. "I shouldn't," I say. "I've been trying to stay away from sugar. It only makes me feel jittery."

"Nonsense." Natalie gently prods me toward the cookies. "Depriving yourself at a time like this isn't going to help anything. You need something to help you feel better."

I take a cookie and take a small nibble. My eyes go wide a moment later. "These are delicious!" I exclaim before taking another bite, this time a larger one. My appetite has been in the shitter lately, but even I have to admit how tasty these things are. I don't know if it's because I'm starving, but I swear they're the best cookies I've ever eaten.

"Aren't they?" Natalie beams proudly. "They're a customer favorite. I can hardly keep them on the racks. Within twenty minutes of putting out a fresh batch, they're gone."

"What are they made of?" I have to ask; I'm still marveling at how rich and sweet they are.

Natalie crosses her arms, her eyes twinkling. "Can't tell ya. It's my super secret recipe."

I savor the taste. I'm really loving this cookie. "I figured you would say that."

Natalie winks. "You know me."

I close my eyes, relishing the delicious flavor assaulting my taste buds. "My God, I always knew you could bake, but never this good." My eyes pop back open as something occurs to me. "Wait a minute, a customer favorite?"

"I took over my grandma Eva's bakery," Natalie explains. "I now run Sweet Morsels Bakery fulltime."

I'm shocked. I had always pictured Natalie going to law school, settling down after a few years and having a bunch of babies. I didn't think she'd stay in town. "You're kidding!"

Natalie shakes her head. "Nope. Grandma Eva got too old to run it and wanted to retire. Since mom was too busy with her daycare business, that left me to take the reins."

"Wow," I say, impressed. "That's amazing. Head of your own business at twenty-three."

"Ain't it?" Natalie agrees. "I never thought that I'd be doing something like this, but here I am." She frowns, as if a sudden unpleasant thought occurs to her. "It's not all cupcakes and ice cream though."

I finish chowing down the delicious treat. Unconsciously, I grab another and pop it in my mouth. "What do you mean?"

"I didn't inherit the business for free. I owe grandma Eva fifty grand."

"Mmm," I say, shaking my head.

Nat nods. "And if that's not bad enough, I also took out a loan to buy the house right around the corner from the bakery so I could oversee the shop. So I'm up to my eyeballs in debt."

The word 'debt' brings up my own worry. Before my stepfather died, I took out a large student loan of forty grand to cover living expenses while I get my master's. And as massive as that debt is, it doesn't even include the student loans I have from my time in undergrad. At the time, I wasn't worried because daddy assured me he had the money to help me pay for it. Now he's gone. My heart twists with pain. I shouldn't be worrying about money. But it's there in the back of my mind. I feel guilty even thinking about it.

"But I'm okay," Nat says quickly at my frown, as if afraid I'll fall into pieces at any more bad news. "Business is brisk, and within a few years I should own the shop free and clear."

"That's good," I say absently, still munching away. Nat's right. The cookies are helping. Maybe I'll just eat the whole fucking tray. "How's the town been otherwise since I've been gone? Anything change?"

Nat shakes her head, watching me. "Nope. Still the same ol' same ol'."

I'm not surprised. Everything looks the same. The town, the people. This church, the exact same one mom used to take me to for Sunday school every week until she passed away. It still looks to be in the same condition since I last saw it. I can still remember the days mom and I used to walk up the steps. When daddy would come, they'd playfully swing me back and forth, holding my hands as we entered the iron-wrought doors.

As I gobble down cookie after cookie, tears burn my eyes and I have to push away the memory. I'm so fucking tired of crying.

"That's enough, Lizzie!" Nat hisses, snatching the next

cookie out of my hand, breaking me out of my recollection.

"Hey!" I object. "That was my last one."

"Right," Nat growls.

"You're the one who told me to eat them," I point out.

"I told you to indulge a little, not eat the whole damn tray!"

I open my mouth to protest, "I didn't eat the whole--" I stop and stare in horror at the cookie tray. Of a dozen, only four are left. Eight. I'd eaten eight cookies without even realizing.

Shaking her head, Nat stuffs the cookie she'd taken from me into her mouth. "Look Liz, I know this is a terrible time for you, and it might seem insensitive to say right now, but I am not going to let you develop any kind of bad habits in order to cope with Turner's death, do you understand me?"

I stare into Nat's face. She looks so serious while chewing that cookie I burst into giggles. "Yes, Ma'am." My laughter draws curious glances from people around the room. A few give me sympathetic looks as if they're thinking my giggles are a fit of hysterics borne from my grief, and start making their way over. I quickly morph my smile back into a frown. *Oh God. Here they come.*

"Good," Nat is barely able to say before she's swept out of the way by a throng of well-wishers.

Before I know it, I'm overwhelmed by everybody talking at once.

"It's a shame about your stepfather, he was one of the best men this town's ever had."

"How are you doing, Lizzie?"

"We're so sorry for your loss."

"Did you know your father was dying?"

"Who's going to watch over the house while you're at school?"

Nat looks on with sympathy while I'm being mercilessly interrogated. She knows I can hardly tolerate some of these people, and I'm just trying to keep it together.

Luckily for me, Nat intervenes right when it feels like I'm about to pass out. "Okay, that's enough," Nat says sternly to the group. "Lizzie's really tired and would like to go inside the chapel to see her father before sitting down."

She grabs me by the hand and begins pulling me toward the chapel doors.

"Thank you," I whisper with gratitude as we leave the group behind.

Nat shakes her head. "No problem. I'm not even you, and they were about to give me a stroke."

I let out a dry chuckle.

My legs are trembling like jello as we enter the chapel. The crowd seated inside goes silent as I enter the room. Though it's the last thing I want, several people get up to greet me in the middle of the aisle. Some give me sad faces, and tell me everything will be alright, that God will take care of me. Others take my hand and tell me they're sorry, while others embrace me and put on an act of crying.

By the time I make it down the aisle with Nat, I feel like

I'm being suffocated. I can only hope the service ends quickly. I don't know how much more of this shit I can take.

Then I see the coffin.

Oh daddy, I cry inwardly. *I'm so sorry.*

There he is, lying in front of me, devoid of color. Lifeless. My legs feel as if they're going to buckle as I walk over to the coffin. I peer down into daddy's face. He looks rested. Peaceful. Still, I can hardly take looking at him. He's gone. Never coming back.

Slowly, I touch his hand. His skin feels cold as ice.

I can't take it anymore. I lose it. My shoulders shake as I sob uncontrollably. Somewhere in the back of my mind, I feel anger. I promised myself I wouldn't break down. But here I am, bawling like a baby.

I hate it. I hate that the vultures can see me crying, that they can see my pain.

All I want to do is go home, curl up in daddy's favorite chair and take in the smell of his cigars. If I could, I'd lay there for days, talking to him, remembering all the good times. But I know I can't.

He's really gone.

At some point, I don't know when, Nat wraps her arms around me and leads me over to my seat. She's rubbing my back and quietly shushing me. I'm handed a handkerchief, which I gratefully take to blow my nose.

The procession has begun, and people are beginning to line up near the coffin to view my stepfather.

"Are you okay?" Nat asks, her eyes filled with concern.

"I'm mad at myself," I say angrily, wiping at my nose.

Nat frowns. "What on earth for?"

"I promised myself I wouldn't break down."

"Don't be. You're only human."

"Yeah, I know I am, but some of these people aren't. I gave them the show they've been waiting to see."

Nat glances scornfully around the room. "Look, don't worry about them. If there's anyone here that's happy to see you cry, then they can lick my asshole."

Even I have to laugh. She's ridiculous. I roll my eyes, but I have to admit, I do feel slightly better.

After I pull myself together, I dare a glance around the room. No one seems to be visibly showing glee at my breakdown, but I know better. I catch a few tight smiles and waves as my eyes scan the room, and I'm about to turn back to Nat when my breath catches in my throat.

Who the hell is that?

There's a man I don't recognize, but he's staring at me. To say that he's handsome is an understatement given his chiseled bone structure and slender, but muscular physique. His short dark hair is a little longer on top and styled in a way that makes it seem messy, yet polished. Like he just woke up looking that fucking hot. He's dressed in a black suit I'm sure cost a couple grand; he looks like he stepped right out of GQ magazine.

Underneath his hypnotic gaze, I'm suddenly feeling self-conscious of how I look. I'm sure with all the crying I look a hot mess. It annoys me that I even care at all. My dad is dead. Looking good is the last thing I should be worrying about. Still, I can't help it. I wipe under my eyes and take in a steadying breath.

"Who's *that?*" I'm forced to ask Nat against my will.

Nat looks around the room until her eyes fall on the handsome gentleman and they light with recognition. "Oh," she says casually. "That's Liam Axton. Your dad's neighbor."

A jolt of shock runs through me. Daddy's neighbor? Nat has to be mistaken. "You mean he lives on the corner, right?" I clarify. "I can't believe the Bernards would have moved from their home. They've lived there all their lives."

Nat shakes her head. "No, I mean he literally lives next door to your dad's house. In twenty-two Wyoming."

I can't help it, but I'm fucking floored. The house at 22 Wyoming was my dad's rental property. It's right next door to our family home, 20 Wyoming. Growing up, he said it was his cash cow and vowed he would never get rid of it. How could he have sold it to this... stranger?

I'm struck silent by this revelation. I steal a glance of Liam. My heart jumps in my chest. He's still staring at me. Hard. Boldly. His eyes seem to be assessing me, burning into me with an intensity I find unnerving.

It suddenly feels very hot in the room, and there's only one question on my mind.

Who the fuck is this guy, and how the hell did he know daddy?

Chapter 2

Liam

I don't know why the fuck I'm here. *The law office of Allen Douglas, Esq*. I'm alone in this cramped office, waiting on the lawyer to come back in here. I wanna get this formality over with as soon as fucking possible.

My eyes dart around from his desk to the old dusty bookshelves, and I want to get the fuck out of here. I need to get away from people. The funeral was enough to make me bolt, but I owed it to Richard.

I already said my goodbyes and laid him to rest, but I had to attend. I can't deny that part of the reason I went was to see *her*. Elizabeth.

He talked about her constantly. Day in, and day out.

Everything reminded him of her in some way. I know he had regrets about not telling her everything. I told the old man he should've let her know. She's a grown woman, and she deserved to know the truth. He was a stubborn man though. He refused to let her see him as he lost more and more of himself. It's not my place to say he was wrong for doing it, but I don't know that I could've kept it from someone I loved.

So she constantly weighed on his mind. I've heard more about her than anything else from the old man. I feel like I know her. When I saw her crying over his coffin, it broke my heart to see her in pain. I guess I can see why he didn't want her spending weeks crying over him. He couldn't stop the inevitable, but he tried to protect her from it until the end.

I wanted to comfort her and tell her how much he truly loved her.

But that's just not who I am. And even though I know all about her, she doesn't know shit about me.

I almost did it though, just because I fucking wanted to. I almost walked up and took her in my arms and shielded her from all those prying eyes. She didn't need them watching her break down like that. I could tell it was bothering her. If it wasn't for her friend being there with her, I would've stepped in. She needs someone. I don't know why I feel so strongly about it, but I want to be that someone.

I make a point not to show emotion around anyone. Acting on emotion gets you killed in my line of work. But she looked so fragile and so damn torn up. Her pain called to a part of me I hardly know, one I rarely even acknowledge. I wouldn't have been able to help myself. I don't protect people; in fact, I do the opposite. But she's different.

I have a feeling she would pushed me away, even if she wanted me to hold her.

A humorless laugh huffs from my chest. If she did, that'd only make me want to hold her more.

My dick stirs in my pants and I feel like a damn pervert, but imagining all the ways I could comfort her has me craving her touch. She's gorgeous and curvy. I can just imagine how she'd feel in my arms. I'd pull her into my lap and kiss every inch of her body. I'd take away her pain and make her forget. That's what I want.

Fuck, my dick's hard as steel. I groan and adjust it before anyone comes back in.

What the fuck is wrong with me? I run my hands down my face and through my hair. I crack my neck and push down all the shit I'm feeling. I'm used to doing that, ignoring whatever bitch emotions are getting to me. I just need to get this reading of the will over with. Then I can move on and get back to the way my life used to be before Richard showed up.

I have to concentrate on work. That's what I need to do. I need to get back to my office and get my shit straightened out.

Instead I'm in this tiny office, waiting on this reading that should have nothing to do with me.

I told that old man not to leave me anything, so for the life of me I don't know why I'm even here.

I purse my lips and realize she should be here soon. His Elizabeth.

I'm in a leather wingback chair, and I settle back before taking my phone out of my pocket. At least I can give his daughter her house back.

He never should've given it to me in the first place. I'm not sure if she'll sell it or rent it out like he used to. Shit, she might even sell her family home that's next door for all I know. Whatever she wants to do, it's up to her.

I wake my phone up and look at the time. *Time for this shit to be over and done with.* I've got a few emails and some texts I need to respond to.

It's only a few more minutes until the door behind me opens, and I'm quick to put my phone away and sit up straight. I take a look over my shoulder as the old lawyer rounds the desk and sits in his chair.

Elizabeth closes the door behind her with a soft click. She stills for a second when she sees me, caught by surprise. But she seems to ignore me more than anything else. Her eyes are on the empty chair to my left.

Her long hair barely moves as she walks slowly to the seat and settles in without a word. She leans down to set her purse on the floor and runs her fingers through her hair. I can just barely smell a hint of vanilla and something else, something sweet. My eyes roam her curvy body as I take her in.

I can't help it.

Our eyes meet, and there's nothing but animosity in hers.

That sweet, sad vulnerable look that was in her eyes at the church is fucking gone. Maybe I imagined it. Or maybe she just doesn't like the fact that I'm here at her stepfather's will reading.

That's not my fault though, so she can get that dirty look off her face. I push down my irritation and give her the benefit of the doubt.

She pulls her long hair over one shoulder and nervously twists it around her fingers.

Her pouty lips are turned down into a frown, and her eyes are a bit puffy. The sight of her still so worked up over her stepfather's death makes my heart clench. She's in so much pain.

He said she used to light up his world with one look. But those baby blue eyes aren't filled with any emotion that conveys happiness.

"My condolences," I offer her in a low voice so I don't startle her. She bites down on her plump bottom lip and turns to look at me. She noticeably swallows and bites out a small thank you.

She's tense and unhappy--I get that. But I didn't anticipate her being so cold to me.

Maybe she's pissed I'm here at all. I have to keep reminding myself that she doesn't know me. I feel like we have a connection that's just not there.

Shit, it's not like I want to be here. Usually I'd blow this kind of shit off; I have more important things to do. But if Richard wanted me here, then I'm here.

Fuck, I was with him every day until he died. I could use a little sympathy, too.

I close my eyes and clench my jaw, hating that I even had that thought just now.

I only knew her old man for a few months. Yes, his death was like a bullet to my chest, but I knew it was coming and he wasn't my father. This isn't about me.

If this is her way of dealing with his passing, then so be it. I'll be her punching bag. I can do that for her, and for him. My foot taps on the ground as I wait to get this over with.

"I know you're dealing with a lot right now," the lawyer says as he reaches across the desk and places a wrinkled hand on top of Elizabeth's hand. "I'm so sorry for your loss." He sounds sincere, and I have to look away and down at the floor for a second. My heart sinks a little. The old man is really dead.

She turns her hand over and grips his like it's her lifeline. For some reason, it pisses me off. I want to be the one giving her that comfort.

But she doesn't know me. I let the anger roll off of me. If he's making her feel better, that's all that matters.

I grip the armrests and sit back. I must be worked up more than I thought over Richard's passing. I don't like it.

"All right, let's go through this as quickly as possible, shall we?" Allen raises his bushy white eyebrows and gives Elizabeth a pointed look.

She squeezes his hand once and sits back, taking a deep breath. She lets go of his hand and lets hers fall to her lap. My eyes catch the movement and my fingers itch to reach out and take her hand in mine, but I don't. I clasp my hands together and wait for the lawyer to get this shit over with. Whatever the old man left me, I'll be more than happy to keep as a reminder of him.

Maybe it's an old watch or a trinket, I don't know. Whatever it is, I'll pocket it and move on. Knowing him, it could be his favorite DVD. I huff a small laugh thinking about it. It puts a smile on my face, but then I remember where I am and I feel like an asshole. Neither of them seem to notice though.

"Let's begin. Richard Francis Turner's Last Will and Testament." The lawyer shakes out the pages and starts reading down the lines, completely oblivious to the fact that Elizabeth is stiff at his words. She's not crying or breaking down like she was at the funeral, but I know hearing those words shook her up. She's not alright.

Allen's words turn to white noise as I watch her clutching her necklace and staring straight ahead with a grim look on her face.

If Richard could see her right now it would fucking kill him.

I usually don't think twice about other people's pain.

That's life. But watching her trying to hold herself together is breaking something inside of me.

Suddenly, her composure changes into confusion and then anxiety.

I look back to the lawyer, trying to pay attention to whatever he just said.

"Hmm." Allen looks lost as he goes through the pages. He flips through them and repeats back what he just said. "It all goes to Mr. Axton."

My forehead pinches as I take in what he's saying. That can't be true.

"All?" *All of what?*

"Everything Richard owned or is in his name, with the exception to the family home, 20 Wyoming and its contents, is to be given freely to Mr. Liam Axton. This includes all other properties, and financial investments, and all the remaining balances in all of his bank accounts. The house, 20 Wyoming, and its contents is to be given to his only surviving heir, Elizabeth Turner." My body goes cold as he says the words and then looks back up at me, waiting for a response.

"What? No!" Elizabeth grips the chair with both her hands before standing up so fast she nearly sends it flying backward. The chair rocks on its back legs before gently settling.

"That can't be right!" She shakes her head. "Daddy wouldn't leave me with nothing."

"I'm sorry, Lizzie," Allen says, looking back down at the

papers in his hand and gripping them harder, wrinkling the pages. He looks back through them as though he read them wrong. "The deed and title for your family home have been put in your name, but all other belongings have been left to Mr. Axton."

So all he left her was his house, the one right next to the one he gave me, but nothing else. What the fuck?

I remain still, and I struggle to accept this is even real. It must be a mistake. She's right, there's no way he wouldn't have left everything to her. He loved her. He wouldn't have done that to her.

"This man didn't even know my father!" Elizabeth points her finger at me for emphasis and chokes on her words as tears prick her eyes.

I reach up for her hand to calm her down and try to explain as I stand, but she rips it away from me. Her wide eyes look at me with worry, and I put both my hands up in surrender.

Her breathing is coming in frantic pants; she looks like she's on the edge of having a panic attack.

I sit back down, not knowing what to do. I don't want to make her angry, but she sure as shit doesn't want me to comfort her right now.

"I'm sure there's been a mistake," I say evenly and calmly. She looks like a wounded animal. My heart hurts for her, so I let the offense slide. *She's just hurting*, I have to remind myself.

"Yes," she says in a high-pitched voice as tears roll down

her face. "There's a mistake."

"There is no mistake; it's all been left to Mr. Axton."

The room is quiet for a moment. Why the hell would Richard do that? I open my mouth to let them know I'll give it all to her. I don't need his money. I hadn't expected this either. I wanted to give the house back to her, too. But before I can say anything, Elizabeth turns all her anger on me.

"Who the hell were you to him? What'd you do, threaten him?" she says accusingly. That really fucking pisses me off. I'm ready to beat that ass of hers for talking to me like that.

"Whoa! Whoa!" I don't like that she thinks so little of me.

He told me not to tell her everything that happened. He doesn't want her to know about the shit he did when his insurance wouldn't pay up for his treatments. Richard confided in me. He put the house in my name without me knowing. He did this bullshit with the will without telling me. And on his deathbed he made me promise not to tell her that he kept all this from her.

I don't know what he was thinking, but if he wanted his only daughter to fucking hate me, then mission accomplished.

"I don't want it," I say simply, ignoring her eyes boring into my head with hate.

My heart twists with pain. I don't want her to hate me. What the fuck was Richard up to, doing this shit? "There's obviously a mistake."

"Obviously." Elizabeth sits back down and leans forward,

looking back to Allen. "If... *Mr. Axton*," the way she says my name makes me cringe, "doesn't want the inheritance, then everything's fine, right?"

"Well, there are some legal issues we can work out." Allen has a tense expression on his face as he looks between the two of us.

"Good, because that's *obviously* a mistake." Her voice hardens as more tears fall down her cheeks. "He didn't know shit about daddy."

That's it. Something inside of me snaps. I was planning on just letting this all go, but the way she's looking at me with pure hate is just not gonna work for me.

I want comfort, too. I want her to give me a god damned chance.

"I want a date," I say, and both sets of eyes whip over to me.

"Fuck you!" Elizabeth sneers. "I'm not for sale, asshole."

That mouth of hers is pissing me off.

I gotta get up before I do something stupid.

She's making me wanna pin her ass against the desk and settle her down the best way I know how.

Without another word, I walk out of the office in a mix of rage and sadness. I storm out, ignoring her screaming at me, and Allen trying to calm her down. I walk straight out to my car to get the fuck out of there. I'm mostly just confused though by the time I swing my car door open and settle down in the seat.

I grip the leather steering wheel and twist my hands. My

heart's racing, and I just want it all to stop. I hate this pain in my chest that just won't let up.

What the fuck was Richard doing giving it all to me?

I told him he didn't owe me. I didn't help him out for the money. It wasn't about that. At least to me it wasn't. I hate to think he even thought that about me.

And now his baby girl fucking hates me.

I clench my jaw and start up my car.

I'm not letting this go. She needs that money. I know she does.

She's gonna have to sit down with me and show me that sweet side I know she has if she wants it. I don't care if that makes me a dick. She brought this shit on herself.

Chapter 3

Lizzie

"There must be something wrong," I insist, holding back an ocean of tears after the handsome bastard storms off. "This can't be right." I don't care if I pissed him off, but even as I think it, my heart sinks. I don't want to piss anyone off. I'm just so damn tired of crying and being in pain. And then this? I don't understand it. Why would daddy do that?

Allen looks at me from under his bushy white eyebrows and shakes his head. "I'm sorry, Miss Turner, but the will is right here, clearly in your stepfather's handwriting." Allen slides the crumpled papers across the desk. "See for yourself."

I snatch it up, causing Allen to mutter an ominous warning, "Careful with that. If you damage the will, Liam can hold you accountable."

Fuck Liam.

Ignoring the old fossil, I scan the document. Sure enough, it's daddy's handwriting. I'd know his distinctive scrawl anywhere. My heart starts pounding like a sledgehammer, and my head spins. My breathing becomes ragged and I feel like I'm going to faint.

How could he? I wail within the depths of my mind. *How could he do this to me?!*

I can't believe it. This can't be true. I want to pinch myself, make sure I'm not stuck in a nightmare.

A total stranger! He left everything to a total stranger!

I can't figure out why on earth he would do this. He knew that I'd taken on massive debt. Debt he had promised to pay so I could live a better life. Then he goes and dies and leaves everything to some random cocky bastard with no relation to him?

What. The. Fuck.

I'm hurt. And beyond fucking mad. To say that I feel betrayed doesn't even begin to express how I feel. My body heats with anxiety, and I don't know what to think about anything.

"He can't do this," I find myself protesting. I want that smug bastard to come back here so I can claw at his arrogant mug. "He can't withhold my inheritance like this!"

Allen reaches across the desk and gently pulls the will from my hands. I instantly regret not ripping it up in his face. Who gives a fuck if Liam takes action against me? The bastard doesn't deserve anything. He didn't even know my father. "I'm sorry to tell you this Miss Turner, but he most certainly can. Liam Axton is the sole heir to your stepfather's estate and he isn't legally obligated to share anything with you, even considering your close relationship with Richard."

I stare at Allen's lined face for a long moment, feeling sick to my stomach. My mind races, searching for a reason why my father would do this to me. What could I have done to deserve such a terrible punishment?

Be a shitty daughter. Every inch of my skin pricks with a chill at the thought. Was I really? I loved him. I should have told him more often. No, I should have showed him. I loved him so damn much. How could he not know that? He was my world.

After all, where was I when my daddy was dying? At school, too busy with my studies to care about keeping in frequent touch with the man who had loved me as if I was his own biological daughter. A man who had died heartbroken and alone, without me to care for him.

Maybe I do deserve this.

I can't take it anymore. I burst into tears, my shoulders shuddering violently from powerful sobs.

I'm so sorry, daddy, I cry inwardly. *Had I known you were sick, I would never have gone so far away for school. Never! I would've stayed at home and taken care of you. Really, I would, daddy. You must believe me!*

I rock back and forth in my seat, the pain crushing my

heart. "I wish I had known," I cry, tears pouring from my eyes. "I wish I could take it all back!"

Allen must think I'm going mad with grief, but he gets up from his seat and comes around to my side. "There, there, child," he coos, patting me awkwardly on the head. "Everything will turn out alright."

I continue to sob and Allen is forced to wrap his frail arms around me, letting me cry on his shoulder.

After what seems like an eternity, I sob my last sob and I'm able to pull away. My cheeks burn with embarrassment when I see Allen's expensive dress shirt is soaking wet from my slobber and tears.

"I'm sorry I got my snot all over you," I sniff, wiping my nose with the back of my hand. I'm such a pathetic mess. But I don't care.

Allen brushes away my worry with a dry chuckle. "You'd be surprised. You're not the first person to break down in my office after a will reading, and you most certainly won't be the last." He reaches across his desk and grabs a couple of tissues and then hands the bunch to me. "In fact, I'm just happy there wasn't any violence between the two of you," he says, as I take the tissues and blow my nose. "I've had to replace my desk at least ten times."

I look at him through bloodshot eyes. "Seriously?" I say and sniffle.

Allen nods. "Usually will readings deteriorate quickly when

certain family members find out they've been left out of the will. I've actually had all-out brawls take place in my office."

I shake my head before blowing my nose again. "That's crazy."

Allen makes it back behind his desk and I feel a twinge of guilt. The poor old man is going to have to smell my slobber all the way home. "Indeed. I find that a death in the family always brings out the worst in people if they think they can end up with something of value."

"Isn't that the truth," I mutter, sitting there feeling numb. I really don't know what to do. I'm heartbroken I've been left with nothing. Something occurs to me. "Do you know if my stepfather knew Liam at all, like *really* knew him?"

Allen shakes his head. "Sorry, I do not."

I frown. It all seems so strange to me. Why would daddy hand over his will to someone he hardly knew? Unless... he really knew him?

He couldn't have known him, I think to myself. *I never saw this guy while growing up at daddy's. He has to be some last minute actor that showed up when daddy grew vulnerable.*

Maybe that was it. Maybe daddy had come down with a sudden onset of dementia, forgotten who I was. Then this Liam character had taken advantage of him. The idea makes my chest burn with anger, though it seems an unlikely scenario. Still, it makes me feel uncomfortable even thinking about it.

I shake my head. It's impossible. I talked to daddy fairly often. That's not it. I feel ashamed for even thinking it. But then again, daddy never mentioned Liam. Who the hell is this guy?

I'm full of confusion and grief, and thoughts of Liam are doing things to my body I'd rather not admit to. *A date.* Did he really say that? I take in a short breath, thinking about doing it. It's just a date, and it's with *him.*

My eyes glaze over as my mind goes back to the funeral and I remember the way he looked at me. Like he wanted me. Like he needed me. Desire burns in my lower stomach, and my cheeks redden from heat.

Allen clears his throat. "Miss Turner?"

I jump in my seat. "Uh, yeah? Sorry," I say, my face on fire. I quickly grab my purse and stand up. I think it's time to go home. "I thank you so much for your service, Allen. I'll be going now."

Allen gives me a nod. "Should you work out something with Liam, I'd be glad to offer my advice."

I touch a hand to my chest. "Thank you. That means a lot to me." *But I won't be doing shit with that bastard, except busting his ass for being a filthy thief.* I walk over to the door and place my hand on the knob. Before I open it, I say in parting, "Sorry for ruining your shirt."

"It's no loss." Allen grins. "I've got thirty more just like it at home."

On the way back to the home I grew up in, my father's

home and now the only thing I have left of him, I keep running through different scenarios in my head. Liam forced daddy to will everything over to him. Liam drugged daddy and made him sign the will over to him. Liam blackmailed daddy and made him sign over his estate.

Each scenario fills me with rage. But not toward Liam, just at myself. There's no way any of that is true. But still, who is Liam? And why did daddy leave everything to him?

Something is absolutely wrong with this scenario.

Whatever Liam did, I intend to get to the bottom of it. I'm not going to let this man get away with what's rightfully mine. I vow that Liam will pay with everything he has if I find out there was any foul play involved in my father's death.

As I pull up, I spot Liam's car, a red fucking Porsche, in the driveway next door. I stare at the car angrily, as if willing it to blow up from my gaze alone.

I'm going to find out who you are, Mr. Asshole, and what you did to make daddy leave everything to you, I think to myself as I glare balefully.

Enraged, I jump out of my car and slam the door. I stomp across the yard, my yard, and to the front door. Balling my fist, I pound on the hard wood like a maniac. It's been raining off and on since the funeral, but right now it's cold and my knuckles hurt as they slam against the wood, but I'm just happy to feel anything at all.

I only get in several thumps before the door swings open

so fast that I almost punch Liam in the face. Good.

He moves to the side, easily avoiding my wild swing. "Whoa! There's a doorbell, you know."

I hate to admit it, but I go weak in the knees at the sight of him. I can't figure out why. He's dressed in the same outfit he had on at the lawyer's office, except now his shirt's unbuttoned down to his chest, showing the hard, tanned skin underneath.

God, he's so fucking handsome, I think to myself.

Slowly, I lower my hand and glower at him, though I feel desire twisting my stomach. I hate how it makes me feel. This guy, this *fraud*, is my enemy, yet I can't help but notice how good-looking he is.

How is that even possible?

"Yes, I know there's a doorbell!" I snarl indignantly.

"Then why didn't you use it?" he asks with a cocked brow. It makes him look even sexier, and that only pisses me off more.

"Maybe because I didn't want to." I say nastily.

"I see. You just came here to yell and call me an asshole some more," he says with a twinkle in his gorgeous green eyes. It's almost if the bastard is looking forward to a showdown with me.

I ignore his playfulness. "What did you do to him?" I demand in the most accusatory tone I can manage.

The corners of Liam's lips pull down into a frown. He's mad now. *Good*. "What do you mean, 'do to him'?" His voice is lowered and all traces of teasing are gone.

"You know exactly what I mean." It takes everything in me

to keep my voice level and not let it crack. Just the thought that he did something to daddy makes my body tremble with anger.

"No. Sorry, I don't." He holds my gaze, daring me to suggest something.

Bastard.

"You should be ashamed of yourself!" I snap angrily. "Taking advantage of a dying man!"

Anger flashes in his beautiful eyes like a violent storm. "Are you fucking serious right now?" he growls. "I was a good friend of your stepfather's, and had nothing but respect for that man."

"Bullshit!" I spit out the word. "Why should I believe you? You're a fucking liar!" I don't even think about what I'm saying, I just let out my rage.

"Who the fuck are you to tell me I'm lying, huh?" He takes a step toward me, towering over me in an imposing manner. I tremble slightly, but stand my ground. "You weren't there to see how close we'd gotten."

You weren't there. His words hit me like a punch in the gut. I almost double over from the pain it summons.

"So knock it off with that bullshit, okay? I didn't do shit to your stepfather, or make him do anything against his will. But I don't give a fuck if you believe me or not." There's hurt in his voice, but more than that, there's anger. And it pisses me off. I'm the angry one here. I'm the one who lost her only family.

Unthinking, I lash out, my hand whipping his head to the side. "Fuck you," I whisper.

I hear a guttural growl. Next thing I know I'm up against the wall in the foyer, right next to the door, my hands held above my head. "You shouldn't have done that," his deep voice rumbles in his chest, his breath hot on my face. "You should really be careful with the way you speak to me." He glares at me with a look that is murderous, yet drenched with desire.

I struggle against his hold on me. I don't know why I bother; his biceps are bulging, corded with toned muscle.

He keeps me rooted in place easily, staring at me with fire in his eyes. "You need to settle down. Your mouth is going to get you into trouble."

I tremble beneath his gaze, practically spellbound by his intensity. Below, I can feel his hard, throbbing cock pressed against my lower stomach. I'm breathless, feeling it pulsate against me, and my temples pound from my racing pulse. My nipples pebble. Seriously, I can probably give Madonna and her cone bra a run for their money right now.

Fuck. My panties are soaked. I'm embarrassed, and I have to close my eyes for a moment to calm myself down.

"Let me go," I order when I finally feel in control again. I try to sound strong, commanding, but my words come out painfully weak.

He shakes his head and keeps my gaze. "Nope. I think I'll hold you here until you check your attitude."

"You can't do that," I say, my breathing ragged. I try again to tug free from his powerful grip, but I might as well be trying to move a mountain.

"Sure I can." He presses into me a little harder and I can practically feel his heartbeat pump through his massive cock.

Dear God. My pussy clenches with need. The thought of him fucking me right here, right now, races through my mind. And shockingly, I want it. I want him. I am seriously fucked in the head.

Seriously, the close proximity to his hard body and throbbing cock is making me tremble with insatiable need.

I can't believe this. This is the man that stole my inheritance from me. Get a hold of yourself, Lizzie!

"I know you want it, too," he continues, bringing his lips dangerously close to mine. "In fact, I bet that pussy is soaking wet for me right now."

My heart flutters in my chest. The bastard is right. I'm going to need a new pair of panties.

"Don't flatter yourself," I croak. I hate how weak I sound.

Liam grins in response. "You sure about that? How about you drop those panties and prove that I'm wrong?"

It's crazy how much I want to please him. I actually consider doing it. The thought of feeling something other than this hatred and sadness is tempting. My lips part with the need to kiss him. Luckily, a loud sound from outside, like a car door slamming shut, breaks me from the lust clouding my better judgment.

This is a line I can't cross.

"Get your fucking hands off me," I say with as much force as I can muster. This time tears prick my eyes and I break eye contact with him. I need to get out of here and away from him.

He knows I'm serious.

"Fine," he says as he slowly lets me down. He keeps his hands on me until I'm balanced and I think about shoving him away, but I don't need any more physical contact or threat of *punishment* from him.

I sulk as I head to the door and turn to face him to say one last thing. "I don't care what you say. I'm going to find out what you did. And when I do, you're through."

I turn and tromp across the yard to my family home, the shitty mood only bringing my mood lower. I can't believe this fucking asshole is right next door. I wish I could put more distance between us, but I can't. I struggle to get the key into the lock and I fight the urge to scream out, feeling so helpless and pitiful. By the time I get inside, I'm soaking wet from the cold, spitting rain. I slam the door closed and lean my back against it, my breathing ragged.

I'm so angry. I'm angry at being attracted to such a bastard. More than that, I'm angry that I have no idea how I'm going to find out how he knew my stepfather. I need to know who that man is. I just don't know how to find out other than asking him. But after today, I know I need to stay far away from him.

Chapter 4

Liam

I feel like shit. I was harsh with her, and I shouldn't have been. I know she's upset. Shit, they just put him in the ground today.

She may think I'm some crook, but if she'd stop hating me for one damn minute she'd see what a mistake she's making.

Her anger and the way she's been talking to me are starting to affect me. I didn't expect that. I was curious before, but now I'm close to being fucking obsessed. I've got a hard-on that's just not going down. Maybe that would shut her up. I huff a laugh thinking about her down on her knees with those plump lips wrapped around my cock. She'd probably do it just so she could bite me. I wince at the thought and walk back to the living room.

If she wasn't Richard's baby girl I'd make sure I fucked this broad out of my system. I run a hand through my hair and walk over to the boxes I was putting together. I've gotta pack everything up.

I grab the clear packing tape from the coffee table and make sure the bottom of this box is secure. I've got a lot of shit over here. I didn't even realize that I'd practically moved in here. It's been nearly three months. I guess I just slowly moved things over here.

To this shitty little house. Well, not shitty I guess. It's old though and small compared to my place.

Richard didn't have anyone though. He was too damn stubborn and he outright refused to tell Elizabeth anything. He didn't want help, but I wasn't gonna let him die in that house all alone. I couldn't let that happen. Not after what happened with my own father. I wasn't gonna just walk away from him.

I wanna tell her everything. I saw the hurt in her eyes when I said that shit about not being there. I didn't mean for it to come out like that. She has to know that. I don't want her to think I was there for him when she wasn't. Even though it's true. It's not fair for her to think that way.

He didn't even really want me there. Well, at least that's what he said. But he never sent me away, and he was always happy to have the company. I remember how even toward the end, he always prepared coffee for us. Stubborn bastard.

He always had to beat me to it, even when things got to the point where he could hardly do a damn thing for himself. He never wanted her to see him deteriorate like that.

I throw the tape down on the hardwood floor and cover my eyes. I'm not an emotional man, but I remember the way he talked about it. How he said he'd never put her through that.

He had a hospital bed in the living room. By the end he was hooked up to machines, and the stubborn man still wouldn't tell her. The last conversation they had, I was there at his side. I was waiting for him to tell her so she could at least say goodbye. But he didn't.

I take a deep breath and steady myself.

It gets to me though.

Richard reminded me of my own father. I was young when my parents got in the car crash. I remember my pops in the bed at the hospital though.

I thought he was gonna make it.

I didn't understand how he could survive the crash, only to die a few days later.

Shit, Richard even looked like my pops.

I remember when he came into the office to put in his first bet. I did a double take. He was wearing faded jeans and an old flannel shirt just like my old man would've worn. Richard had greying hair that was thinning out some, and his hands were worn from all his years of honest labor.

We see a lot of clients day in and day out. Even though

most only show up when they have to pay. They're never happy then. Instead they're usually scared and wishing they could take it all back.

I'm not gonna lie, I make good money off their bad bets. I run the business with my brother and cousin. I guess it's a family business, considering my uncle's the one who raised the three of us and taught us the ropes.

When the clients come in to place the bets though, they're giddy. Happy and excited. They feel like they can't lose.

But not Richard. I'd seen that look on his face a few times before, and I could tell right away what it meant. He was a man who *needed* the money.

I almost didn't take it. I watched as he placed the bet with Zac, my brother. He was obviously new to placing bets, but he pulled out a piece of paper with his notes on it. He'd done his research at least.

When he lost, he came in to double down. He'd placed a shit bet. He looked worse off than he'd been before.

Tyler brought me in to see what I wanted to do about it. Zac takes the bets, but Tyler makes sure they pay up. And I make sure shit runs smoothly. It's a nice system we have going. Tyler could tell something was off with Richard, too. When you don't come in with the money you owe us, there's a problem. Tyler knows how to deal with that shit, but the desperation coming off Richard was something else.

I told the old man that making bets he couldn't pay would

get his legs broken. Richard just gave me a smile and told me I'd get my money either way. He just needed the money fast.

Colon cancer's a bitch. And expensive.

His days were numbered; it was already spreading. He said he had to try though. His insurance disagreed. They gave him less than twelve weeks and said the treatments probably wouldn't do anything. So they refused to pay. But he wasn't giving up hope. He had to live. He had a daughter who needed him, and he wasn't going to go down without fighting.

I don't listen to sob stories. I don't care about personal shit. But for some reason I had to help this guy out. I grabbed the cash from the vault and handed it over to him without thinking twice. Two hundred and twenty grand.

At first he refused. He tried giving it back to me. That's just the kind of stubborn asshole he was. But after I gave him an ultimatum, the cash in my hands or nothing, he finally left with the money.

The next day he came back with the deed to a house and the key.

He said the real estate agents couldn't sell it in time, but if he could, he'd have the money he needed, easy. But he said after he was gone, I could sell it and it should be worth a bit more than the money I gave him.

I could see the pride in his eyes vanish when I shook my head and told him I didn't want it. It had hurt him to be given the money. So I grabbed the deed just to make him happy.

He nodded and shook my hand.

I didn't know what to do with it. I don't need shit from anyone. And I sure as hell don't need a house in the suburbs.

That night I drove by the address on the deed and saw him there. It took a good ten minutes before I realized it was the house next door that he'd given me.

Maybe it's because I could never do anything for my pops, I don't know for sure, but that night I stayed in the house and made sure I saw him every day that followed.

The doctors were right; the treatments didn't help, and I was there when the life left him.

It fucked me up pretty good. One minute, the machine was beeping, the next it was just a single tone.

I wish he hadn't made me promise not to tell anyone. Especially Elizabeth. She'd feel so much better if she knew the truth. I know she would.

I told that old bastard he should tell her. But he looked me in the eyes and said he didn't want her to remember him like that.

Tears prick my eyes and I have to stop thinking back to him and all that shit. I place my phone in my pocket and try to get back into work. I need a damn distraction from all this. But that's fucked, too.

Ian's making threats and being a pain in my ass. He's our competition in a way. And he's sorely losing his clients to us, because of his shit business tactics. My cousin, Tyler, should know to take care of this shit and nip it in the bud. Intercepting clients and making deals to pay off their debts with me is a no-no, and Ian knows it. I already know I'm gonna have to step in before shit gets out of hand. I don't feel like it though.

I'm so damn exhausted. I get up and make my way upstairs. I just need to sleep this off. All this stress and no outlet to relieve it is making me tired beyond belief.

I remember Elizabeth's soft body against mine. I fucking want her. She tempted me, and now all I can think about is punishing her tight pussy. I'm surprised with how much restraint I had.

As I collapse onto my bed upstairs, I can faintly hear Elizabeth. Her childhood bedroom is right across from my bedroom. Only ten feet or so separates our houses. But from my window, I can see straight into hers. I know because I've looked out this window staring at Richard's house, waiting for this all to end so many damn times.

I hear another small sob and it breaks my heart. She's crying again. Fuck, it hurts to know she's right there. If she didn't want to hate me so much, I could take away her pain, mine too, if only for a moment. It's better than having to deal with all these shitty emotions.

I wanna go over there.

I wanna ease her pain.

I want her to take mine away, too. I already know how

good she'd feel.

I wanna make this right. I don't know why this is all fucked. But I'll make it right. I shouldn't have been such an asshole. She doesn't owe me shit. It was selfish of me to do that shit today. I did it out of anger and pride, and took advantage of her mourning her father. I'm such a fucking prick.

First thing in the morning, I'll let her know it's all hers and that I'm gone.

I'm a bad man, but I'm not so bad that I wanna hurt her like that.

She's too good for me anyway.

I should've known better. I never should've chased something I can never have.

CHAPTER 5

LIZZIE

I *can get through this. One step at a time.*

I take in a slow, trembling breath, fighting back the pain twisting my stomach. After a moment, I let out a sob and bury my head in my pillow, muffling my cries. Smothering the screams.

It's so hard being in this house. Memories of daddy keep flashing through my mind, filling me with grief-tinged nostalgia. I can still see him now. His weathered, but charming smile. The gentle way he always treated me. How dearly he loved me. Fuck. I'm even seeing mom, too. It's been so long since that pain has felt so raw.

I'm trying hard to keep myself together. But I feel like my soul's been shattered into a million tiny pieces.

Fight it! I shout in my mind, trying to deny the tidal wave of pain surging through my limbs, making me want to wallow in my grief. *Be strong for daddy!*

That's what daddy would want. He'd want me to fight, be strong for him. Not indulge in my misery. I have to do it. I have to make him proud.

After what seems like an eternity, I'm able to quiet my sobs, though the tears and pain remain. I sit up on my bed, sniffle, and wipe at my tearstained face. I look around my room, noting that everything is exactly how I left it. Ryan Reynolds posters adorn the pale pink walls, and there's a big fat ass purple Barney stuffed animal in the right corner of the room. I thought it was funny to keep him, but now all it does is remind me of how my father won him for me at a carnival. It fucking hurts.

Emotion threatens to overcome me again, but somehow, I manage to push it back.

Last night wasn't good. Not at all. I thought I'd be productive. I thought with how angry I was at Liam I could handle going into daddy's room and packing up some of his things. I was wrong, for two reasons. One is that I'm definitely not ready to say goodbye yet. The second is that daddy had already done it. Tears leak from the corners of my eyes, but I don't bother to brush them away. Daddy knew he was dying.

He cleaned up everything so there wouldn't be as much work for me. The tears come harder, and I press my palms to my eyes. It hurts so much. I wish he'd spent his last moments with me and not doing shit like that.

It takes a moment for me to calm down. A long moment.

"Pain, pain go away," I whisper, "Don't come back for any day."

I sit there for a while, staring at my posters. Numb all over. Then a thought occurs to me.

Maybe I should just give Liam what he wants. I'll have to sell this house. I know I will. I have so much debt, and no job. I haven't had any income while I've been in school. Grad school doesn't leave time for anything else other than hitting the books. School. I huff a humorless laugh. That's a pipe dream now.

The idea of giving in to Liam is so appalling, I almost let out a bloodcurdling scream of fury. Seriously. It pisses me the fuck off to have to rely on the handout of a stranger. But the stakes are high. If I can't dial back my ego, I'll lose my house. My father's house. The one thing I have left of him. And if I give in to Liam, I'll lose my pride. Pride's the only thing I have left at this point.

I have to decide which is more important. And that's an easy choice. I can't let go of this place. I can't say goodbye like that.

A date will give me a chance to know him more. And I do want that. I need to figure out who the hell this man is. I wish I wasn't so attracted to him though. It makes things complicated.

Shit. *I hate it.* I hate how he makes me feel, how he makes me want him. It's not right. It's not right how I want him to bend me over and fuck me like I'm his. How I want him to own every inch of my body.

I should tell him to fuck off. To go to hell. Fight the will and contest it. Take him to court, sue him for everything he's got. But deep down, I know it's not worth the fight. The will is ironclad. With the high cost of legal fees, I stand to lose more than I'll gain.

The smug, handsome bastard has me in the palm of his hand.

And he so knows it, I think angrily.

If I accept his offer, I don't know how I'll get through it. Good God, how can I survive being around a man I want to kill and fuck, all at the same time?

This house. I need to focus on keeping this house and just being able to live. I have no money without doing this.

That's it. *My inheritance.* What's rightfully mine. What he stole from me. If I keep my mind on that, I should be good. He'll never get to lay a finger on me. One date, and then it's all over.

I wipe my face one more time and rise from my bed. I've got dried tears and slobber all over my face and nightgown. A cool shower will do me some good.

I make my way into the bathroom. I grab a towel and place it on the sink. Then I disrobe and look in the mirror. A haggard-looking young woman looks back at me. Even with a pound of foundation on left over from yesterday, I can see the bags under my eyes. Days of no sleep and constant crying spells are really showing.

Hopefully I'll look more refreshed after a long, hot shower.

I turn away, open the shower stall and turn the knob. I place my hand under the stream and wait for the water to turn lukewarm. When it's tolerable, I step inside and close the door.

I let the water hit my face and drench my hair, imagining it washing away my pain and worries. I grab the pouf hanging off the showerhead and lather it with a lavender-scented body wash. I lift it to my nose and inhale deeply, focusing on soothing my battered soul.

As I begin to lather my body, naughty thoughts about Liam begin invading my mind. Suddenly, I'm back in the moment of being pushed up against the wall, his cock pressing against me. Desire burns through my lower stomach and my legs tremble slightly as my pussy begins pulsing and clenching uncontrollably. I let the pouf drop and the water rinse everything away.

Unconsciously, I begin rubbing my pussy, imagining Liam here in the shower with me, his hard cock pressed against my lower stomach and demanding entry.

"Oh fuck," I moan, the image making me dizzy with lust.

I move my hands faster between my thighs, rubbing my

throbbing clit in a circular motion. Pleasure courses through my limbs as my nipples stiffen like stone.

God. I want him here now. Taking me. Fucking me.

My breath quickens, becoming ragged. I slump against the shower wall, moaning and groaning. In my mind's eye, I imagine his chiseled body drenched with water, thrusting his powerful hips against my ass, plunging his huge cock deep inside my needy pussy.

Pressure builds inside of my core, threatening to explode.

I'm going to cum. All over his big fat cock.

Gasping, I snatch my hand away from my aching pussy.

What the fuck are you doing, Lizzie?

I'm shocked at how close I've come to having an orgasm. Fantasizing about Liam, no less. *My enemy.*

My thighs are trembling, and I'm shaking all over. I'm not sure if I'm shaking from my near-orgasm, or how frightened I am at just having lost control. Probably both.

Ashamed, I quickly finish my shower and then step out into the steamy bathroom.

As I dry myself off, I vow to forget what just happened. It was just a mistake. An anomaly.

It will *never* happen again.

Done drying off, I slip into an old favorite pink bathrobe. I locate my blow dryer under the sink and plug it in. I still can't think straight; I'm just going through the motions. I flip my hair to the side and am about to turn the blow dryer on when the doorbell rings.

"Shit," I mutter, wondering who it is. After a moment, I figure it's just a well-meaning family member, come to check on me. I have neither the temperament, nor the patience to deal with that shit right now. I'll just ignore it. Whoever it is can come back later.

I press the power switch, and the loud hum of the dryer fills the room. I purse my lips when I think I hear the doorbell ring again. I turn the dryer off for only a second and sure enough, there's another chime. I ignore it, turning the blow dryer back on and let the hot air run through my hair, enjoying the sensation. I can faintly hear the doorbell ring again, this time repeatedly.

Whoever it is, isn't going away anytime soon.

I blow out a sigh of frustration and turn off my blow dryer.

I'll just go answer the door and tell them I can't deal with visitors right now. I check my appearance in the mirror. My hair is wet and disheveled. I look a mess. But I really don't give a rat's ass. The person outside has no business harassing me like this. I can't wait to give them a mouthful.

I rush out of the bathroom, down the hallway, and down the stairs. *Ding-dong. Ding-dong. Ding-dong.*

"Just a minute!" I yell in annoyance. Good God. Whoever's outside is going to regret doing this. Don't they know I'm grieving for my father? Why would someone be so rude at a time like this?

Breathless, I reach the door and snatch it open, ready to do battle. And then I know why. My heart does a backflip. *Liam.*

He's looking like he stepped straight off a modeling shoot, dressed in simple blue jeans and a buttoned white shirt that shows off his corded biceps. His hair is slicked back, and his chiseled profile makes my heart flutter.

His eyes widen as he sees me, wet from my shower, only clad in my flimsy robe. His gaze travels down my body, to my breasts and then my long legs which stick out from the slit in my robe. In an instant, he catches himself and brings his eyes back to my face.

Too late. I saw him check me out. Hard nipples and all.

My cheeks burn with embarrassment and I pull my robe tighter around myself and cross my arms across my chest to hide my erect nipples. "What are you doing ringing my doorbell like a maniac?" I demand angrily. "Come to assert your male dominance some more?"

Liam swallows hard and then clears his throat. "I came over to tell you something." He doesn't seem at all bothered by my bitchy put-on in the least.

Images from the shower flash through my mind, causing my pussy to throb. *Sweet Jesus.* "Tell me what?" I ask, casting those naughty thoughts back to hell where they belong. My voice sounds strained. I hate it. And I feel guilty. If he only knew what I'd been doing in the shower before he showed up.

Whatever he has to tell me must be pretty damn important,

leaning on my doorbell like that.

Liam pauses as if thinking about what he wants to say. "That I'm sorry about how I treated you yesterday," he says finally.

My jaw nearly drops to the floor. "You? Sorry?" I snort with derision. "That's a good one."

Liam carefully keeps his eyes on my face. "I'm serious. I shouldn't have come on to you like that. You just lost the most important man in your life, and were just acting out your emotions. I should've had enough empathy to realize that instead of behaving like an asshole."

I'm at a loss for words. Seriously. I've been building up Liam as my enemy since I first learned who he was. Our last two--and only--exchanges didn't go well. And now this? I don't know what to think.

Yet looking at him, I don't doubt his sincerity. He appears to be truly sorry.

"Well, uh... that's nice of you to say," I mumble, not knowing how to take this sudden turnabout in behavior. "Thank you for telling me." I'm practically whispering, and I can't even look him in the eyes.

The corners of Liam's kissable lips curl up into a soft smile. "Just nice?" he asks.

"Yeah," I say. "Sweet. Really sweet of you." I clear my throat and add, "I'm sorry, too. I was out of line." It hurts to admit it, but it's true. I just want to hate someone. I want someone to blame. And Liam's a good target.

Liam chuckles. "You're really cute, you know that?"

My cheeks burn again. "I've been called worse."

"Only by fucking idiots," Liam growls.

I'm taken aback. Liam has not only apologized to me, but now he's taking up for me. Now I'm really not sure what to make of all of this.

For a moment I'm stunned, unable to come up with a suitable response. I have too many conflicting emotions. Anger. Sadness. Lust. To make matters worse, all I can think about is how it felt when Liam's hard body was pressed up against mine.

I look Liam in the eyes. I see sincerity there. And... desire. He wants me. I know it. I could invite him in right now for a passionate tango, and I'm sure he'd jump on the chance. I just can't let that happen. I need to have some self-control.

I begin to part my lips to reply... I don't know what. A part of me wants to demand he sign over my inheritance to me, another part of me wants to yell at him to go away, and yet another wants me to let him have his way with me.

I bite my tongue, not trusting myself to speak. With all the dirty thoughts and emotions raging through me right now, I'm afraid of what might come out. Besides, I'm not sure if Liam is trying to play me. By giving in to my desire, I could be playing right into the palm of his hand.

I have to be on guard with this man. I don't know him at all.

"I didn't mean to disturb you when you were so..." He

pauses as his eyes flicker down my robe, and a shiver runs down my spine. "Indisposed." He gives me a cocky grin, signaling he's lying. Of course he'd meant to disturb me with the way he'd spammed the doorbell. But at this point, I don't care anymore.

Suddenly, I feel as if I've made up my mind about my situation. I just hope it won't end in disaster.

He runs his hand through his hair and turns to look back at the house next door, *his* house, and then starts to say, "About that date--"

Heart pounding, I blurt out, "About that." I cringe at the note of desperation that enters my voice.

Liam turns back to me and appraises me with a furrowed brow. "Yeah?"

Dear God, Lizzie. I hope you don't live to regret this.

I take in a deep breath and reply, "I think I'm willing to take you up on that offer."

Chapter 6

Liam

That was unexpected. I don't know how to feel about this broad.

The last day or so, I've gone back and forth with how I feel about her.

The way she said she accepted my offer should tell me everything I need to know. This is a business deal for her, nothing more. We go out, and I give her everything that was left to me. A simple transaction.

I don't fucking like that. That's not what I want. I want to go out with her, the real her… shit. I twist my hands on the steering wheel, and grip it tighter. My knuckles are white.

I'm a liar. I wanted to fuck her. That's why I said that shit.

I know that's why.

I was hurting, she was hurting. And she was pissing me off. She didn't even try to get to know me. My heart pains in my chest. Yeah I wanna fuck her, but I want her to know that I did care about her old man. My relationship with him was short-lived, but I know the pain she's going through.

I fucking need someone, too.

I park my car in the office parking lot and look up at the highrise. It's a sleek steel building with large, dark glass windows. It's intimidating and masculine. And I own the entire building. I had it built just for our business.

It's an odd feeling going from the cozy rundown house that Richard used to rent out and then handed over to me, to walking into this building.

It feels colder and lonelier than it ever has before. I don't like it.

I don't talk to anyone on the way in. I don't need to. Most don't know who I am anyway. I'm just a man who rents the top floor, or so they think. They don't need to know what I do, or why I do it. My clients come in through the back of the building via an elevator strictly for my business' own use. Not this one. I prefer coming in through the lobby and taking in the condition of the place. I'm a silent partner, I am in all my investments, but I like to check in and make sure everything runs smoothly.

Everything is separated between my business and the

other businesses here, even the parking lot. It keeps things neat and clean. I own everything, and that way I can control it all. This is why my brother and cousin need me.

We have high-end clients because of me. It doesn't stop some of the Joe Schmoes from coming in and risking all they have on their favorite team because it's their lucky day, but it does make this business a commodity.

I stand by the elevator and walk in, trying to shake off my feelings about Elizabeth agreeing to my proposal. It wasn't meant as a business deal. I stretch my shoulders slightly and breathe out my annoyance. A few people walk in after me and I wait for them. I stand quietly at the back of the elevator. There are doors behind me and I have one of only three keys that will open them.

The bell dings, and the elevator cart comes to a halt.

I adjust my crisp white shirt sleeves and crack my neck as I wait for the two women in pencil skirts to stop gabbing and get off. There's only one man left and he's in a nice navy suit with thick blonde hair that's styled professionally. He keeps eyeing me like he's wondering what I"ll be doing on his floor. He thinks I'm stopping on his floor since I haven't pressed another button, but I'm not.

I give him a tight smile as the cart stops on the thirty-eighth floor and he exits. He looks back over his shoulder with one last curious glance as I push the button to make the doors close. I take out the key and slip it in, pushing in the code and wait till it reaches the top floor.

I rock on my heels.

I used to think nothing of this. Going into work was just a daily chore.

I enjoy my job. There's always something to do and new ways for us to improve. But my heart isn't in it today. That's for damn sure.

The doors slide open and I walk into the airy space. It's one large, open concept area. The back wall is covered with 110-inch ultra high-def televisions. There are sixteen of them, spaced evenly on the back wall. The majority of the space is divided into four seating sections with sleek black leather sofas. And in the very back, there's a bar stocked with top-shelf liquor.

I head to the left though, past a buffet station used for catering and walk straight through to my office. It has the same masculine feel as the den. But I like staying in here because it's closed off and soundproof. I don't have to listen to that shit that goes on out there, but they also can't hear whatever it is I'm doing back here.

If Elizabeth saw this, I wonder what she'd think. I doubt she'd think I was a bookie, maybe a party planner instead. Since we do throw what I guess you could call parties. It's a live betting arena. And the thrill of watching it happen gives our clients an aspect to our business they don't get anywhere else.

Every month I get more and more clientele because of

the unique features we offer. And that's a problem for some people, like Ian Dracho. Many of our customers come from him. He's a lowlife who I know for a fact has rigged games to get out of holes he dug himself.

To take the bets, you have to know the odds. You have to be good with numbers and statistics. My brother's damn good at that, but Ian isn't. So he rigs the games, or offers shit bets that only fools would take. I don't blame his customers for leaving him. But he sure as fuck does. And he blames us for taking them.

My ass doesn't even touch the leather in my Herman Miller Aeron chair before my brother Zac and cousin Tyler walk in. The three of us make a good team. I know I haven't been around much lately, and they've been bugging the fuck out of me because of it. I'm not surprised they were on me the second I got here. It's not like we're going to have anyone coming in for an appointment until later anyway, so what else do they have to do other than give me shit.

I sink back into my seat and try not to be irritated.

Zac looks like me, but with a baby face that makes him look approachable and charming. The sharp features only I inherited from our father, well they give you a hint that I may be dangerous. But Zac could fool anyone into thinking he's Mr. Right. He takes the seat across from mine at the dark walnut desk and angles it so Tyler's included in a circle of sorts.

Tyler's all muscle, and that's why he's good at his job.

His broad frame fills up the wingback chair in the corner of the office as he sits back and sets his right ankle over his left knee. He's a quiet man and doesn't say very much. But when he does, you listen and right now he looks like he's got something to say.

"'Bout time you came back." Tyler's voice is deep and has a hint of humor. That, combined with the smirk on his face makes me think he's not quite as upset with my absence as Zac's been.

"You done being on vacation?" Zac asks sarcastically. Yeah. Zac's pissed. I'd spent a lot of time with Richard. I shouldn't have. But what's the point of having your own business if you can't take a break when you need one? Although, I have to admit, it's been a little over twelve weeks since I've had my head in the game, and that's a long fucking time.

I fiddle with the engraved silver fountain pen on my desk. It always sits here. My father used to keep it in his pocket. He liked to say that it was his good luck charm. Always had this damn pen in his pocket... except for the day of the car crash. I'd begged him to let me hold onto it that day when he'd left. Zac was too young to remember, but I'll never forget. "It wasn't a vacation," I say simply before righting myself in the seat and leaning forward. I set the pen back down and straighten it, putting it right where it belongs.

I clear my throat and continue looking my brother in the eye as I say, "Give me an update on the numbers first." The bottom line is what matters. Our expenses are immense and they pay off well. But a small dip one month could mean a decline overall if something's not right.

"Numbers are good." Zac adds, "They're actually a bit up."

My eyebrows shoot up in surprise. "I wasn't expecting that."

"We got in a few more clients that like to have fun more than they care about the bets." I nod my head and smile.

"That's what we want," I say with a cocky grin. We want them to enjoy the experience, so even if they're losing their money, they'll keep coming back.

Tyler huffs a laugh and says, "Gotta admit, I like those clients more." Tyler's more of a bouncer than anything for those clients. For the most part anyway.

Put enough men in a room, add alcohol, and shit's bound to get out of hand. I give Tyler a nod, but turn back to my brother. Although I'm a bit relieved to hear we don't have problems on the money front, there's still some serious shit that needs to be dealt with.

"There's still an issue that needs to be taken care of," I say and gesture to Zac, who's nodding his head like we're on the same page. I'm the problem solver. I fix shit, and I develop our brand. That's my job, and I'm damn good at it. And right now, we've got shit that needs fixing.

"Dracho is a fucking problem," he says flatly.

"I'm gonna need more than that, Zac. How many clients has he taken?" That's really what this is about. He sees us as a threat, and we are, but there's no way he can beat us. Not with the shit operation he's running.

"None of the top earners, but a client is a client and when they owe us, I don't like getting a call from him. He can't reach out to them and take on their debt. It pisses me off." Zac's angrily tapping his fingers against the chair. He's on edge and pissed. He adds, "He's pushing us by doing that and interfering with our business."

I clench my jaw and crack my neck. Zac's got a point, but if the people who owe us go somewhere else looking for a loan, we can't stop them. I look back to the pen on the desk and run the tip of my finger along the engraved lines. It's a habit I have. This is tricky.

The guys are quiet while I try to think of a way to stop this shit from becoming a bigger problem. I'd say we could just stop doing bets with the clients that know of him, but there are a lot that have come to us after dealing with that prick.

"How much of our business came from him?" I ask.

Zac shrugs his shoulders. "How the fuck should I know?"

I imagine it's a lot, considering his name is brought up in our circles with regularity. He's got a right to be mad since we took his business, but if he was better at his job then that wouldn't have happened. That shit is on him.

"The only thing I can think of is requiring the cash up front." I settle on a solution, although I don't really like it.

Tyler whistles in his seat, and his eyes widen. Apparently,

he doesn't like it either.

"We'll lose a lot of business that way, Liam." Zac's right. We would lose a lot of business, but that's the only way we'd guarantee not having to deal with that asshole.

"Do you have any alternatives?" I ask him.

"We could take care of him," Tyler says flatly. It turns my blood to ice. Tyler's father, my uncle, was a member of the mob. It doesn't mean much to Tyler if someone's gotta go, but I don't like it. It's best to avoid that situation in the first place by preventing it from happening. I shake my head and nod at Zac.

"Okay, not our high-end clients. But the others, the ones we know came from him. We're going to require their payments upfront. How much business do we stand to lose from that?" I ask Zac.

Zac looks up to the ceiling and taps his fingers on his knee for a moment before he looks back to me. "I'd really have to check the numbers, but it's probably as high as twenty percent."

I lean back and say, "Problem fucking solved. We can take that hit. Our profit margin can handle that, and it'll get that prick off our backs and out of our territory."

Zac's face finally cracks a smile and he nods, looking at Tyler and then back at me. "Alright, I'll let 'em know."

"We could've used that answer a month ago, Liam," Tyler says from the corner.

"Yeah, well, I'm here now."

"So no more sneaking off?" Zac asks.

I take a deep breath and look away. I don't have to answer to either of them, but I'm not gonna lie to my brother. "I'm going back tonight, actually."

"You moving into that place?" Tyler asks with disbelief.

A rough chuckle rises up my chest, "No. No, I am not moving into Twenty-two Wyoming. I'm giving it back to the old man's daughter."

They know all about him. And for the most part they gave me some time and space while I was away. Zac was younger when pops passed. But they know it took a toll on me.

"Why you going back then?" Tyler asks.

Zac butts in with a smile as he says, "Let me guess, the daughter."

My lips turn down into a frown.

"I'm right, aren't I?" Zac says, happy as a fucking snot-nosed kid in a candy shop. "Tell me I'm right."

"Fuck off," I say with a bit of humor.

"You for real?" Tyler asks.

"I knew it!" Zac slaps his knee. "You're such a bastard, Liam."

I shake my head, not wanting to tell them anything. Besides, it's not like I've been fucking her.

"Who is this broad?" Tyler's asking questions, and Zac's making assumptions. I don't like either.

"No one. Unless you two have any more business to discuss, I suggest you get the fuck outta here." They don't need to know about her. All the stories Richard told me flood back to me. But in an instant they're gone and replaced by that look on her face when she accepted my offer.

She looked so fucking beautiful with her skin all flushed from just getting out of the shower. She's a natural beauty. But she'd look better if she wasn't wrecked from exhaustion and stress. And I could tell she wasn't happy to go out with me.

I want it though. I'm a selfish asshole, so I'm going through with it. A small piece of me is still hanging on to something. I don't know what, and I don't know why.

She thinks I'm bad news, and she's right.

But I just want a taste of her sweetness.

I want her to know me like her father did.

More than that, I want to know the woman Richard was always talking about.

I need to make sure she doesn't regret this.

Chapter 7

Lizzie

I peer at myself in the mirror, staring critically at my figure. I'm wearing a red dress with spaghetti straps that looks nice, but lacks impact. The lush curves I usually enjoy when I'm at a healthy weight are somewhat diminished.

Damn, I think to myself. *Nat was right. I've really lost a bit of weight. But it's not my fault I don't feel like eating.*

Nat has tried everything to get me to eat, with no success. I can't even stomach her delicious sugar cookies anymore.

Still, I like what I'm wearing. It's classy, but it shows off my womanly figure. The weight loss hasn't taken that from me at least.

As I stare at my appearance, I tremble with excitement.

It's been a few days since I accepted Liam's offer. I've expected to see him since then, but he's been gone. I'm all worked up and nervous that he's changed his mind. But he hasn't. And for some odd reason that makes a small part of me giddy.

In a few minutes, Liam will be here. I'm not sure if I made the right decision by taking him up on his offer. I know practically nothing about him. For all I know, his apology was designed to get my guard down so he can con me, like how maybe he conned daddy. If I'm not smart with this guy, I could end up in a lot of trouble.

I need to be careful. I take a deep breath, trying to gather my wits, but my eyes pop open wide as the doorbell rings.

Cursing my luck at not being completely ready, I run out of my room and down the stairs. I make it to the door and realize... *Shit! I have no makeup on.* Thinking quickly, I unlock the door and run back up the stairs.

"It's unlocked!" I yell from the top of the stairs. "You can come in now!" I dart around the corner as I hear the door creak open.

"Elizabeth?" I hear Liam call. It's odd hearing my full name. No one calls me Elizabeth.

"I'll be down in a minute!" I yell from the upstairs hallway, my heart pounding. "Can you wait in the living room?"

Sure." I hear the door close and then his heavy footsteps as he walks through the hallway to the living room.

Thank God.

Five minutes later, I have my war paint on. I'm wearing a light layer of foundation, rosy blush, smoky eyeshadow and a shiny lip gloss. I've done a rush job on my hair, styling messy curls going down the right side of my face, but it's good enough. I make my way downstairs and stop before I enter the living room, anxiety washing over me.

I wonder if he'll think I look good, I worry. For a second, I have the urge to run back upstairs to change outfits and mess with my hair again. *Stop it right now, Lizzie Turner,* I scold myself. *You're going on a date, not marrying the man. Pull yourself together. And this is only to honor my end of the deal he offered and to find out what he meant to daddy.*

A twinge of anger runs through my veins, but it's dimmed. I haven't felt the same about Liam since he apologized. It's harder for me to be angry as the days wear on. But I hold onto it, because without it, there's only sadness.

After a moment, I gather my courage, take a deep breath and walk into the living room. Then I nearly swoon.

Dressed in black slacks and a bright white, crisp dress shirt that's open at the chest, Liam's sitting on the couch, legs planted wide, watching TV. The way he's relaxed there, his hair a bit messy, looking hot as fuck, is driving me wild. Seriously, I've seen guys sit like that before, but he's making an art form out of it. He looks like he owns the place, like he's the fucking king of the world.

The image of walking over and straddling him, smothering

his neck with kisses while his hands roam all over my body run through my mind, making me shiver with need.

Liam seems to sense my presence. He tears his eyes away from the TV and they settle on me. "You look beautiful," he says in a deep, husky voice, not appearing to notice my inner turmoil. Hunger flashes in his eyes as he says those words.

"Thank you," I say softly. "You don't look so bad yourself."

Liam grins.

That's when the theme song on the television hits me. It makes my heart jump. As I walk farther into the living room so I can see for myself, I gesture and ask, "Is that MacBoys you're watching?"

Liam glances at the screen and then grabs the remote, turning the volume down. *He knows how to operate the remotes. They're a pain in the ass. One to turn the TV on and off, another for the volume and a third for the channels. And he knows how to use them. Has he been here before?*

He nods. "Yeah, it is." He seems to sense that him watching daddy's show has gotten to me. I can't help it.

I fight back the tears that threaten to spill from my eyes. "That was daddy's favorite show." It's hard to keep my breathing steady at the reminder.

"Yeah, I know," Liam says in a soft voice. "He's the one that got me hooked on it." He starts to say something else, but then he stops, looking a bit choked up.

Liam sounds so sincere that it's hard not to imagine him

and daddy being friends.

It's just an act, I tell myself. *A ruse just to gain my trust.*

A part of me wants to call him out on it. Call him a liar. Accuse him of making up stories so that I won't go after him for taking my inheritance. Yet when I look at Liam's face, all I see is real, raw emotion. It's easier for me to think he's a liar than to accept he and daddy were friends. Because if that's true, where did that leave me in my stepfather's eyes? And without focusing my energy on hating Liam, my mind goes straight to my father.

"He must have meant a lot to you," I find myself saying. *I can't believe I just said that.*

Liam nods. He clears his throat uncomfortably. "He was a good man." He nods his head, but doesn't look me in the eyes.

I grow silent. I stare at the man I thought was a liar. A man I treated like shit and took my anger out on, rather than hear out.

"Let's go, shall we?" Liam says abruptly. He turns off the TV and stands up. He runs his hand through his hair and I can't help but be slightly distracted.

I should say no. I should tell him I'm sorry. I'm so damn sorry I ever questioned daddy's will. I feel like shit. Daddy left everything to him for a reason. I should just be happy I have this house. Tears prick my eyes, and I wish they didn't because Liam's quick to come over to me and try to comfort me.

I awkwardly laugh and brush the tears away, shaking my

head. I hate how he's seeing me like this.

"I'm sorry I brought him up," Liam says as he starts to reach for me, but then stops.

He doesn't even wanna touch me. I breathe in deep and look at the ceiling with my eyes wide to prevent the tears from coming and ruining my makeup.

"Hey, it's alright." Liam leans in a bit and rubs his hand down my back. I want to lean into his touch. But I know I shouldn't. I feel weak. If I give him an inch, I'll be begging him to take a mile. And that's a mistake. Even with my head clouded in lust and sadness I know that much at least.

I let out a heavy exhale and get ready to apologize and take it all back, but he beats me to it.

"I wanna take you to dinner," he says simply. "Come on, let's just get out and relax." I stare deep into his sparkling green eyes and wonder if I can really do it. *Relax*. Like it's just that easy.

He sees my hesitation and pouts comically before saying, "You said you would; don't back out on me now."

I laugh and sniffle a bit.

"Alright then. Let's go." I give him a soft smile, and something eases in my chest when he flashes a handsome, bright smile right back.

"Perfect," he says and leads me to the door, as if this is his house. As if he's been here a thousand times. I start to think about this house and all the memories it holds and why I'm here, but I shut it down. I take one last deep breath and leave it all behind as we start our *date*.

We walk outside and he holds the door open for me.

"Thank you," I say softly, clutching my wristlet in my hands.

"You like Italian?" he asks smoothly. As though this is easy for him.

"I do." Lasagna is one of my favorite dishes. My mom used to make it a lot growing up. Well, really any pasta dish. Daddy used to say she loved carbs a bit too much. The happy memory turns the corners of my lips up for a moment. Just a small moment.

"Good, because I know the perfect place to go." I'm snapped out of my memory by Liam's words as he opens the passenger side door for me. I give him a small nod and slide in.

He drives me downtown to the strip, a place where the hottest clubs and restaurants are. The entire drive, neither of us talks. We simply listen to the music on the radio. It's hard to keep my mind from wondering if he's even interested in me. We pull into the parking lot of a restaurant called Di-Italio.

I've heard of this place. The cheapest plate is a hundred bucks.

I really don't feel comfortable with a guy dropping several hundred dollars on me on a first date. Especially a guy I'm not sure I trust yet. A guy I'm not sure I really want to be on a date with. I stifle my objections and carry through with the plan. It's just a date. Just one date.

He comes around the car and lets me out. He's being a

perfect gentleman, and I'm doing my best to accept it without feeling like a fraud.

"Thank you," I say softly.

"Of course." His deep voice calms me and settles my worries. He splays his hand on my lower back and leads me to the door. My heart blossoms. I've never been courted this much before. And especially not by such a handsome man.

What's a man like him doing with a woman like me? I try to push my insecurities away. Aren't I worthy of a man like this? A man who admires and respects me? I start to speak, but I can't finish.

As the man at the front entrance opens the door, I turn and face Liam. "I think this is really very nice of you, but--"

He puts a finger to my lips, completely catching me off guard. The act is intimate. And he seems to realize it only after he's done it.

He slowly pulls his finger away and clears his throat.

"I just wanna feed you," he says. "Just sit down and let me meet the daughter Richard always talked about." Hearing him bring up my father makes my heart swell. I search his face for the real reason why he could possibly want to be here with me. But I can't think of any other than he genuinely wants this date.

I nod my head in agreement. I can do this.

My lips part slightly as my heels click on the travertine tiles on the floor of the restaurant. It's beautiful. There's a rustic feel to the decor that seems to take me to another place.

Soft sounds of a soothing violinist mingle with the murmurs of chatter in the large venue. There are sconces on the walls, and candles on the tables that provide dim, but intimate lighting.

The deep reds and off-whites of the linens adds to the romantic feel. It's nearly overwhelming.

"I've never been somewhere so nice before," I quietly admit to Liam, looking up at him through my lashes as the maître d' leads us to a circular booth in the very back. It's in its own corner and it's more secluded here; the noises are even quieter, the lighting even darker.

"Well then," Liam says as he smiles down on me. "You're in for a treat."

Chapter 8

Liam

It was hard to keep a straight face when Elizabeth said she's never been somewhere so nice before. Her father said the same thing when I took him here.

I own this place. Well, technically I own fifty-one percent of it. I'm a silent partner though. It was a damn good investment. And it makes me happy to be able to take whoever I want here, whenever I want. Food's good, and so is the atmosphere.

I'm happy I brought her here. I finally have a moment with her where she's not trying to claw my eyes out.

I can tell something's really bugging her. To be honest, it's a bit awkward. Almost like a blind date. Except that I already know so much about her, and she hardly knows a thing about me.

"Listen," she starts to say, but then a waitress comes with a pitcher of ice water and fills our glasses. The young woman sets the pitcher down gently on the table and presents the menus. She starts rattling off details that we don't need to hear.

She offers some Shiraz for tasting, but I already know what I want. "Could we have a bottle of Screaming Eagle Cab?"

Elizabeth looks at me from the corner of her eyes with a smirk.

"I know it doesn't sound quite right, but it's from Napa Valley and you're going to love it."

The waitress nods her head in agreement and adds, "It's delicious. It'll go wonderfully with whatever you choose from the menu."

Elizabeth gives me a tight smile and says thank you. She reaches for the menu and tilts it slightly. Her lips fall open after a moment and I watch as her eyes go down the rows of items.

I take a sip of water, not bothering to look at my menu. I know exactly what I want. I get the same thing every time I come here.

She purses her lips in disappointment, and I have to ask, "What's wrong?"

Her eyes fly to mine and she shakes her head as she says, "Nothing." She's so tense and obviously not feeling alright.

"I thought you liked Italian," I say simply. I'm not buying

that 'nothing' response she gave me. If only she'd tell me what's wrong. I hate that she's so standoffish. I need to remember she doesn't know shit about me.

She sets her menu down and looks away before looking back at me. "I'm just stupid. I was going to get lasagna. I don't know what some of these other things are." Her voice trails off, and she looks away again, markedly embarrassed.

I reach out and turn her menu over. I tap on exactly what she wants. "It's right here. You'll love it." Finally, her lips kick up and she seems to relax a bit.

"Thank you," she whispers. She reaches for her water and takes a sip. Her eyes still don't reach me.

She's not pissed at me anymore, which is nice. But there's nothing there in its place. She's shy and seems uncomfortable.

I think she needs a fucking glass of wine. As do I.

I take in a deep breath and decide I need to get this weight off my shoulders and just tell her something about me and her father. Something to ease her worries about me. But I'm not sure what to say. I don't want to break my vow to Richard, and I also don't want her to know what I do for a living.

But before I can say anything she turns to me and asks, "So what do you do, Liam?"

Fucking hell. I look her in the eyes as I tell a white lie. Not even really a white lie, just a lie of partial omission. "I have a few investments." I take a drink from my glass as she eyes me skeptically. I can practically see her desperately trying to keep the disdain off her face.

I need to give her a little more than that. "This place is one of them."

Her eyes widen with surprise as the waitress comes back and pours a small amount of the cabernet sauvignon into my wine glass. I take a sip and nod. I already knew I'd like it. I'm just going through the motions.

When the waitress leaves, Elizabeth leans in and asks, "You own this place?" The surprise in her voice is evident.

"Only part of it. I don't do any of the work. I just put in the money and get a return from it each month. Nice and easy." She considers my words and takes a sip from her glass.

"Mmm," she says as she starts to set it down, but then puts the glass right back up to her lips. "That's really good." My chest fills with pride.

"I told you." I give her a cocky grin.

She looks down at the table and then pushes her hair behind her ears. "How did you meet my dad then?" she asks.

I wish she hadn't. I don't want to lie to her, but I don't want to break the only promise I made to a dying man.

"He found me," I say as I start talking without thinking.

She gives me a sad smile and says, "Daddy was good at doing that. He liked to talk a lot."

"Yeah he did," I add. "He was a good man."

She looks up at me like she wants to ask more, and my heart beats faster with anxiety, but she doesn't.

I need to get off this subject and get it on her. Women love talking about themselves.

"So what are you going to college for?" I ask her, even though I already know the answer.

She turns her shoulders toward me and answers, "Well, I'm getting my master's in psychology." She stops talking and looks down at the table. She pinches the tips of her fingers and looks away for a second, but I don't understand why.

"You doing alright?" I ask her. Richard said she was. She could've been lying to him, though I don't think she would have. He said she was doing great and that she'd be done soon. I don't understand her reaction.

She looks back at me uncomfortably. I thought I was making progress with this broad, but every turn I hit a damn brick wall.

She starts to answer but then reaches for the glass and takes a large gulp. What the fuck?

She finally faces me and answers, "I can't really afford to go back... now."

My heart sinks in my chest. I need to put that shit to bed.

"Elizabeth," I start to say, but she flinches like I hit her. I'm thrown off guard.

"No one calls me Elizabeth," she says with a hushed voice.

"Your father did."

"I know." Her voice croaks slightly, and her eyes glass over with tears.

"Hey," I reach out and take her hand in mine and rub

soothing circles on her wrist with my thumb.

She shakes her head and pulls her hand away slightly. "It's fine. Ignore me. I just need a little time." She breathes in deeply.

"It's gonna be okay. I'm sorry, Elle."

She tilts her head and shakes it slightly as she says, "Lizzie." She tries to correct me, but I don't think of her as a Lizzie.

"Lizzie's a kid's name." I like Elle. It suits her. *Elle.*

She considers me for a moment, thinking about something, but not giving me a clue as to what it is. "What were you saying?" she asks, forcing the tears back and putting on a front of calmness.

It takes me a second to think about where I was going with all that, but then I remember. I decide to just go for it, like pulling off a damn bandage.

"Everything is yours. What your father left to me in the will, and the house he gave me. I don't need it, and I don't know why he left it to me. But it's all yours. I called the lawyer yesterday and you'll have it all in your name as soon as possible."

Her entire body seems to sag with relief. She looks back at me with disbelief. I can tell she doesn't know if she really believes what I'm telling her.

"It's yours," I say simply.

It's quiet for a moment before she says, "Thank you." She takes the napkin off the table and folds it in her lap neatly, focusing on it.

"It's yours, not mine. Your father loved you. You were all he talked about. I don't know what he was thinking."

She looks back at me with skepticism and then sadness as she asks, "He wasn't angry?" It throws me off.

"Angry?" I ask her. I don't know why she'd think he was angry with her.

"At me. For leaving, or for not calling enough..." Tears fill her eyes, and she's quick to put the napkin over her face.

I respected Richard. I may have even loved him. But right now I hate him. I never agreed with his decision not to tell her, and looking at her now I wish he'd made things more clear for her. She shouldn't be thinking this shit.

"He loved you more than anything." I don't know how much to tell her. I scoot closer to her in the booth and gently pet her back. "He said you were his sunshine."

A small sob rips from her throat, but she's quick to settle herself.

"I'm sorry," she finally says as she pulls herself together.

"Don't be," I tell her. "You can let it all out."

She gives me a small, humorless laugh and drinks down her water to calm herself. I think about moving away, but I don't want to.

"So, tell me something," she says out of nowhere.

"Like what?" I ask her.

"Anything," she answers. Her big blue eyes look back at me with sincerity. "I just wanna talk."

I'm quick to remember one of the stories Richard told me about her sneaking a bottle of peach schnapps into her room. I tell the story the way he did. He thought it was funny as hell. The entire time she's got a wide smile on her face and her eyes are glassy, but full of happiness. I smile back at her and in that moment it hits me. This is what I wanted. This is what I thought we'd have together.

This is so much better. Almost an entire hour has passed since we've gotten our wine, and my little Elle is really warming up to me. I fucking love it. This is exactly how I imagined it'd be between us. This is how I pictured her.

"Tell me more," I say. She's been talking all night. It's like she's got all these memories, just pouring out of her. I'm happy she's sharing them with me.

"Well, the one time when we were at the dealership, daddy said he didn't like the car." Elle takes another sip of wine. It's her third glass, and after this one I'm cutting her off. Mostly because she's nearly drunk, but also because the bottle's empty. "And the salesman looked so sad. Daddy had been talking about seeing that car for weeks, but when he finally saw it in person, he changed his mind." She moves her hands in the air, talking animatedly.

I grin at her, she's so into this story. She's so cute. "So I felt really bad for the guy, you know? He'd just lost his sale."

"Yeah, I can see that."

"So I started talking up the car to daddy. Saying how much I loved the color, and how the leather seats were nice and really comfortable." She slaps her hands onto her lap, adding, "And they were heated."

I chuckle at her.

"Well, I talked it up so much, daddy bought it." She lets out a small giggle with her shoulders shaking. "He gave it to me a few years later when I got my license." She takes another sip of wine and adds with a laugh, "I hated that damn car. It broke down like eight times."

"How old were you?" I ask her.

Her forehead scrunches up. "Gosh, like fourteen?" She says it like she's asking me. Like I'm supposed to know the answer.

I give her a small laugh and shake my head slightly. "You really are a sweetie, aren't you?" I ask her.

She giggles a little. "Daddy used to say I was sweet as Dixie." Her fingers trace the edge of the wine glass and although her smile dims, it's still there.

"Yeah, you were real sweet to me," I say sarcastically to lighten the mood before picking up my own glass and finishing it off.

She busts out a laugh a little louder than she should. It's a beautiful sound though that fills my chest with warmth. She takes the glass of wine in her hands and runs her fingers along the stem before finishing the glass. That's the entire bottle. I don't even have a buzz, but she's a little more than tipsy.

She needed that wine. That's for damn sure. And a good meal. She ate her entire plate of lasagna, and more than half of the lava cake I ordered for us to split.

She takes a spoonful of the remaining chocolate syrup and half of a strawberry and spoons it into her mouth. Her plush lips close around the spoon and she moans softly. My dick instantly hardens. The date may be close to over, but the night's just getting started.

"Hey, why don't we get out of here?" I ask her. I've got a million things I wanna do with her. A million and one I wanna do *to* her.

Her eyes light up with excitement and she sits up straight, leaning into me. "And go where?" she asks with a hint of excitement.

"Let's go back to my place. We can play some cards." Richard told me how she'd always bug him to play when she was younger. He swore she'd grow up to be a professional blackjack player.

A beautiful smile stretches across her face. I've never seen her smile like that. It looks beautiful on her.

I love it. I love that I put it there even more.

"Yeah, okay," she answers softly. She bats her thick lashes and bites down on the tip of her tongue. A blush rises to her cheeks. "That could be fun."

Chapter 9

Liam

I can tell Elle's buzz is starting to wear off as she shifts in her seat in my car, and I'm thinking she might change her mind about coming back to my place. I don't want that.

I'm driving like crazy to get back to 22 Wyoming. I'd take her to my place, but it's farther away and I don't want to give her more time to change her mind.

I think she'll be happier close to home, too. She'll have an escape if she wants it. Although, my place in the city would impress her more. I wrestle with which place I wanna bring her to, but really, 22 Wyoming is closer, so that's where we're going.

Elle lays her cheek against the seat of the car and says, "I owe you such an apology." Her crystal blue eyes look up at me with sadness, and I don't like it. I don't wanna take a step backward. We don't need to go back there.

"You don't owe me anything--"

"Yes I do," she says as she nods her head and leans forward, cutting me off. "You're just a nice guy, and I was so mean to you."

She's getting all worked up, and I don't like it. I want the fun girl at the restaurant back. And I'm not really a *nice guy*.

She starts going on and I cut her off as we pull up to my place. "Stop it." I put the car in park and grip her chin in my hand so she has to look at me. "You don't owe me anything but a night out."

"It's been really fun," she says haltingly, as if the date's over. My heart pounds in my chest. I finally got her, no way I'm letting her get off that easy.

"Fun's just getting started," I say as I push my door open and walk around her side to open hers. But she's already got her door propped open.

She places one foot on the ground, a bare foot, and gets out with her heels in her hand. I reach for her other hand and she waits a moment before putting her small hand in mine.

I try to lead her around the car to 22 Wyoming, but she plants her feet on the ground and looks over at her family home next door.

"I think I should go home," she says in a small voice. I should've taken her to my place in the city. Damn it.

I keep my expression neutral. "If you wanna, that's fine. I

just thought it'd be fun to kick your ass in a little card game."

Her expression changes instantly. "You think you can beat me?" she asks with a small smile. "Like it's gonna be that easy?" she scoffs, then looks back at her house.

I shrug and say, "I mean, I'm good at what I do." I lean against the car casually, not letting her see how bad I wanna get her inside my place. All through the night I kept picturing her under me. I'm so close. I can't fucking stand it. "Just a drink and a game of cards." I'm lying through my teeth. I want so much more than that.

Elle looks at the ground and purses her lips before looking back up at me and saying, "Okay, just one drink *and* I deal."

I smirk at her. "If those are your conditions, I accept." I already know I'm gonna guilt her into letting me deal. She may look like a hard ass, but she's a pushover. I can practically guarantee this night is going to end with her in my bed.

"I don't know how you're kicking my ass this bad," I say comically as I lean back in the old chair at the kitchen table. This set was here when I moved in. I do know how I'm losing; I've been purposely busting my hands to build her up. She's got all the black chips in front of her, and most of the reds and whites. There's no way she can deny me dealing out a few hands; I'm really working up the sympathy. 'Cause I wanna start betting more than chips.

"I thought you said you were good at this?" she asks me with a sly smile as she shuffles the cards.

"I used to play all the time with my brother." I start to tell her about my own father and how he taught us to play, but then I stop. She doesn't need to hear all that. I don't want her sympathy for my loss just days after putting her own father to rest.

"He used to kick my ass, too." That's true, but Zac's a special case. He's good with numbers and he could kick anyone's ass at cards. She doesn't need to know that though.

"Can I deal this one?" I ask her with a cocked brow. She clucks her tongue, but easily passes the deck to me.

I reach behind me to the fridge. I don't even have to get up, the kitchen's so damn small in this place. I could practically cook a meal while still sitting at the head of the table. I swing the door open and grab a beer. "You want one?" I ask.

She scrunches her nose and shakes her head no. "Oh yeah?" I say in response. "My beer's not good enough, it's gotta be expensive wine?" I tease.

She sticks her tongue out. "I just don't like beer."

"Alright then, you wanna shot?" I ask her. Her buzz is completely gone. I certainly don't mind it, but I wanna push her boundaries a little.

She looks down at the cards before looking up at the clock on the stove. I expect her to use the time as an excuse to get going, but instead she looks back at me and nods. "Yeah, just a small one."

I give her a wide smile and get my ass up to grab a bottle of vodka. That's all I've got. I take two shot glasses out of the cabinet and pour a *small* one for her and a full one for me.

I place hers down and get ready to throw mine back, but she's just staring at the shot glass like it's going to bite her.

"What is that?" she asks.

"Vodka. It's not gonna bite you, Elle." She rolls her eyes and tips it back. She slams the glass down with a scrunched-up face.

"Okay," I say as I sit back down, setting the bottle on the table, "If I win this hand, you do another teeny tiny shot. If you win, what do you want?" I ask her.

Her eyes twinkle with a little mischief. "You wanna up the ante?" she asks.

I smirk at her. "What are you thinking?" I ask.

She bites down on her lip and whispers, "Can it be strip poker?"

My dick has never been this hard. I swear to God if I don't cum tonight, I'll die from blue balls.

"It most certainly can, Elle," I answer with a straight face and she bursts into laughter.

Now I'm regretting that shot. I need to win this hand and every hand after this. But I've still got my wits, and it'll take some time for the alcohol to even hit me. I'm quick to shuffle the cards and deal them out.

She's got a twelve showing with both her cards up. I smirk at her, feeling cocky. This is gonna be an easy win for me. She doesn't take the hit, and sits back like she's not worried. But I know she's gotta be.

I've got a ten up and flip the bottom card. It's a five. Shit, that's not good.

"You gotta take it," she says with a smile on those beautiful plush lips. All I can think is regardless of who's naked first, those lips are gonna be wrapped around my cock. The sooner I get this done with, the sooner I can get what I really want.

I get a seven and bust.

I push the cards to the side, unbutton my shirt and toss it on the floor.

Elle looks calm and collected, but a blush rises up her chest and into her cheeks. I stretch a little and her eyes dip to my chest. She clears her throat and sits back in her seat, trying to act like she's unaffected. I know she likes what she sees though.

I shuffle the cards and grin at her as I say, "You can smile all you want Elle, but that dress is coming off next."

Her cheeks flush a violent red, but she doesn't respond as the cards are dealt.

She gets two face cards. "Twenty, stay," she says with a smug attitude.

I deal myself an ace on top and that sweet smile on her

face falls. I flip my bottom card over, and my dick twitches when I see the jack of diamonds. "That dress has gotta go."

She purses her lips, but slips her straps down and shimmies out of it. I slowly shuffle the cards while taking in those gorgeous breasts. The cards almost fall out of my hands, but she doesn't notice. Thank fuck. That bra needs to come off though. I wanna see those nipples right now. They're hard, and I wanna see them. Right fucking now.

Her chest rises and falls with deep steady breaths as I quickly lay out the cards. She's dealt a sure loss of a hand.

"What's it gonna be?" I ask her with a brow cocked.

"Hit me," she says in a voice laced with lust as she signals a hit and busts at twenty-four.

I expect the bra to fall, but she shifts in her seat and my eyes catch a red lacy pair of panties fall to the tiled floor. I close my eyes and hold back my groan.

Shoving the cards to the side of the table, I deal out what I hope is the last hand.

I smile when I see an ace up for me, and she's got a seven and an eight.

"You wanna see?" I ask her with a hand on my bottom card. I fucking hope it's a ten or a face card. She bites down on her bottom lip and nods. Her eyes are focused on the card.

Ten of clubs.

"Dealer has blackjack," I tell her with my eyes on hers even though I'm dying to look at her chest.

She reaches behind her and then pulls the laced bra away slowly. Her tits are perfect. They're large enough to be held in my hand, and those nipples are tiny little buds with a pale pink color.

I lock eyes with hers and say, "Come here, Elle." It's bold of me, I know it is. But I've been pushing her all night, and she's been with me every step.

All of a sudden she looks nervous, but she gets up and walks over to me, completely naked and looking all sorts of shy. I turn in my seat, and the legs of the chair scrape against the floor. That's all I can hear along with her heavy breathing, and the blood rushing in my ears.

I'm surprised there's blood anywhere in my body other than my cock. It's pressed against my zipper, hard as fuck and ready for her.

As soon as she gets to me, I grab her hips and pull her closer. I stay in my seat and lean forward, taking her tiny nipple into my mouth and swirling my tongue around it. Her head falls back and her hand flies to my hair. Her nails scratch my scalp as she grips on to me.

Her soft moan fills the room, and it fuels me to pick her ass up and set her down on the table in front of me.

I let her nipple pop out of my mouth and plant a kiss on her belly before pushing her to lie down.

She looks at me with wide eyes before bracing herself on the table. "Lie down for me all the way, and put your feet up here."

I tap my hands on the table right where I want her feet and wait.

Her lips part slightly and she's slow to obey, but she does it.

She does what she's told, bending her knees and spreading herself for me. I look down at her pretty little pussy and instantly start leaking precum. She's so fucking wet, she's glistening. I don't hesitate to push two thick fingers inside of her. Holy fuck, she's so tight.

She gasps and her back bows, but I'm quick to push her hip down and hold her in place. I pump my fingers a few times, and her pussy clamps down. Fuck, she's going to feel so good. I stroke her G-spot until her legs are trembling. My eyes stay on her face the entire time. Her eyes are closed, and her lips parted in utter rapture. She needs this. She needs me.

"Cum for me." She shouts out her release on my command, and her pussy tightens and then spasms on my fingers. Fuck, yes. I pull out and taste her. So fucking sweet. I groan as her heavy breathing starts to settle.

I move my hands to my zipper and kick off my jeans as I lean down and get a better taste of her. I suck her clit in my mouth as the jeans drop to the floor. They make a loud noise as they fall and it makes Elle's head pop up. I look back up at her with my mouth still latched onto her clit, but she's shaking her head.

What the fuck? I release her and wipe her juices from my mouth as she tries to say something, but her voice is too low. I'm guessing she wants a condom. That's fine for tonight, but I want her raw as soon as fucking possible. If she wants paperwork I'll have it faxed over for all I care. I don't give a fuck. I need to feel her pussy pop on my dick with nothing in between us.

"What's that?" I ask her, pulling my dick out of my boxers and stroking it once.

She shakes her head again and then leans back, looking at the ceiling. "I don't... I don't..."

I raise my brows and lean forward a little. "I can't hear you, Elle. You don't what?"

"I don't want to have sex." She spits out the words fast and refuses to look at me, her eyes still focused on the ceiling.

What? Why the fuck... What? I can't even put a coherent thought together.

"I'm sorry, I just..."

I sit up and give her a little space and she closes her legs. Fuck, I feel a weight on my chest. I pushed too hard, too fast. "Nah, it's okay." I gentle my hand on her thigh and give her a soft smile. I don't want to scare her off; I'm afraid I already have though.

"I could," she says as she shrugs a little and doesn't look me in the eyes. "I could do other stuff?" She says it like it's a question.

"Let me take care of you again." I look down at her pretty pussy and stroke my dick. I'll take care of both of us.

"You don't have to," she says in a small voice. Her forehead is pinched and I know she's anything but happy about telling me no. I get it though. That's alright. I can wait.

"I want to," I tell her and then kiss her thigh. "I want you to ride my face this time."

She looks back at me with surprise, and I keep my eyes on her as I lower my tongue to her pussy again.

I take a lick and wait for her to relax. She does instantly. Good girl.

I don't waste a second.

I shove my face in between her legs and lick up her tight cunt, spearing my tongue into her pussy. My fingers grip her ass tightly to keep her in place.

"Oh yes!" she screams out as her back bows. That's it. She just needs a little more to get her going. This time I'm not letting her get off so easy. I smile into her pussy at my little joke and then suck on her clit until she's writhing under me and moaning my name.

My chest fills with pride. That's right, my name. I wanna hear her screaming it soon as she cums on my dick.

I flick my tongue across her clit and pull her ass closer to me. "Ride my face," I command her as I push my tongue flat against the top of her opening and her clit. She rocks her hips, and her hands move to her breasts. Oh, fuck yeah.

I watch her and stroke myself under the table as she pinches her nipples. Holy fuck, she's so hot. I stop paying attention to her pussy and just suck on her clit as her body trembles.

Her toes curl, and her legs push inward. I've gotta take

my hand away from myself to push her leg back, and as I do she screams out my name and pushes my head into her pussy, rocking herself shamelessly against me.

It's the sexiest fucking thing I've ever seen. My balls draw up and I cum instantly and without warning. I reach my hand down as quickly as I can to try to catch the hot streams of cum as her arousal leaks down my face.

My spine tingles, and I groan into her pussy as more comes out of her. The vibrations from my groan send a shiver up her body. She slowly lets go of my hair, and her body goes limp.

Holy fuck. I came just watching her get off. Watching her cum is by far the sexiest fucking thing I've ever seen. But there's no way I am letting her know I got off under the table. I'm quick to get up and shove my dick in my boxers as I step out of my jeans. Her head turns, and she starts to move.

"Stay." I give her the simple command without thinking. Shit, I don't think she'll like that. I expect her to react to it with attitude 'cause who the fuck am I to talk to her like that, especially when she doesn't even wanna fuck me, but she just lays back down. I wash my hands in the sink and grab two handfuls of paper towels. One of them I run under the warm water.

I bend down quickly as I get to the table to wipe up the floor as fast as I can. I don't want her knowing what I'm doing. As I get up, my head hits the table. Fuck! That hurts. I hit it hard. I wince and grab my head where the pain is pulsing.

She pops up as I try to play it off, and her eyes go wide

with worry. "Are you okay?" she asks.

I'm still holding my head, but I answer. "Yeah."

"Did you hit your head?" She looks confused, and her eyes are looking on the floor.

"Yeah," I answer and don't elaborate. She laughs a little and lays back down, but she's looking at me like I'm a lunatic. At least she's smiling.

As I wipe between her legs, she starts to look a little uncomfortable again and says, "I'm sorry." Her mouth opens to say more, but I stop her.

"Don't you dare apologize. I fucking loved it." She has no reason to be sorry, and I don't want her to have any regret over this.

"I can--" she starts to say as her eyes look to my boxers, but she doesn't know that's already been dealt with.

"No, you don't need to do that." Her eyes go a little sad, and she bites her lip.

"I'll wait for you, Elle." I give her a small kiss on the lips. "When you're ready, I'll be here."

Chapter 10

Lizzie

The next day all I can think about is Liam down in between my legs, eating my pussy out like a starving man. The sensation of his powerful jaws clamping down on my clit had been mindblowing. I'm still getting shivers from the out-of-this-world orgasm he'd given me.

Yet one thought keeps bugging me. *I should've gotten him off.* Like, what was I thinking?

That I didn't want to give myself to him yet.

It's true. I don't want to play my cards too fast, even with how hot he makes me. But I wanted him. And I'm the one who initiated things with the strip poker. I was playing with fire, and I knew that. Still, I can't understand why he didn't want me to at least return the favor. It doesn't make sense.

Thinking about it, it makes me feel self-conscious. Was it because I was drunk? Maybe, but I wasn't sloppy, falling-on-my-ass drunk. I was just a little tipsy, and I definitely knew what I was doing. I didn't even wake up with a hangover. If he was so concerned about that, he wouldn't have gone as far as he did.

For a moment, I wonder if I made a mistake in playing the poker game with him at all, but then brush the feeling away.

It was definitely better than just coming back here, running upstairs and crying my eyes out in my bed, I think to myself. *Anything would be better than that.*

Looking around the cold, empty house, I feel incredible sadness, which confirms I made the right decision.

I really should stop worrying. I'm reading too much into the situation. Liam provides a useful distraction from all the pain and grief I'm going through. An outlet for my emotions. I need him.

Or maybe he's the last thing I need.

I need another opinion, I think to myself.

I pull out my cell and dial up Nat. It's been a while since I've dated. It's just not something I'm really comfortable with. I don't know why. I'm just not interested. Well, I wasn't. But now I am.

"Hello?" she answers, sounding out of breath.

"Hey Nat!" I say, trying to sound cheerful.

"Lizzie! I'm so happy to hear from you!" She sounds so chipper and like she really is happy. It brings a smile to my face. I'm really lucky to have a friend like her. We've been apart for years, but every time we see each other, it's like we pick right back up from where we left off.

"Are you busy?" I ask.

"No, not at all. I just need to put a fresh batch of cookies in the oven and then I can talk. One sec."

I feel relieved. "Ok."

I wait and hear the sound of metal banging in the background. I lie back on the sofa and laugh at what I've done. It's like I'm at the psychologist's office. Nat's my shrink. I roll my eyes. I am so fucked if she's the one who's going to walk me through this. I can't help but silently laugh.

Nat is on the phone again a minute later. "Back. What's up?"

I pause before telling Nat my dilemma. Would she think less of me if she knew I was fooling around with a man so soon after my daddy had died? I subconsciously start biting my nails as my smile falls. I hadn't even thought of that. I think back to my studies, and I know it's normal to seek out a pleasurable distraction when you're upset, especially when mourning. But that doesn't change the fact that she may think worse of me.

"Hello?" Nat presses when I don't say anything.

"I need your opinion," I breathe out. I need someone to talk to. I can't keep all this in anymore. I take a deep breath. I need a friend. And that's what she is. She's a good friend.

Nat sounds intrigued. "Opinion on what?"

I freeze up again, worrying Nat will not like what I have

to say.

"Lizzie?"

Screw it, I think to myself. *Nat isn't going to judge me. I hope.*

Taking a deep breath, I tell her everything. About the house and Will, our date, the poker game and our foreplay.

"And he didn't want you to, like, at least... take care of him?" Nat asks when I'm done.

I feel relieved that she didn't immediately jump to judging me.

"No," I say. "And I don't understand it." The self-conscious feeling increases. I hate it.

"I don't know, Lizzie. I don't think there's anything wrong with that, if you ask me. In fact, I would kill for a guy who got me off and didn't expect anything in return. Lord knows, I fucking deserve it with how hard I work." She snickers. "Maybe I should start offering sugar cookies in exchange for some mind-blowing cunnilingus."

I laugh. "You're cray cray."

Nat continues, "I'll put a sign out front that says, 'Will Bake For Sex'."

After a short laugh I reply, "I've tasted your cookies. You might get a lot of action with that offer."

"If only!" Nat snorts. "Really though, you better tattoo your name on that tight ass of his. Claim him before anyone else finds out and there's a line of chicks waiting around the corner for him."

"Please," I say and laugh. "I can't do that." That's not what we are. There's nothing about him that's screaming commitment. My brows furrow, and my heart sinks a little. I'm not even sure if we're dating. Is that a thing still? Do people still call it dating?

Nat snorts again. "The hell you can't."

"Not happening," I repeat. "But seriously, I still can't believe what happened. Yesterday, all I wanted to do was go on a date with this guy so I could fulfill my part of his deal and move on. Instead, I wind up laying naked on his table."

"There are worse things in life," Nat says. "In fact, I think you need Liam right now, Liz. He might be just what you need to help you get through..." Nat's voice trails off, but I know exactly what she means.

"Maybe," I say softly. Maybe. Possibly. God! I hate how wishy-washy I feel about this situation.

"So shouldn't that solve it?" Nat asks. "Spend more time with him, get to know him more before going further. Maybe it's a good thing you two didn't have sex."

"That's the problem. I'm afraid to get to know him."

"Why?" she asks.

"I'm afraid I might find out..." *He's a fraud*, I finish in my head. I don't want to believe he is. But I still don't understand how he inherited everything. I put a hand over my face, feeling like a greedy bitch. Seriously, why would daddy do that? But Liam is giving everything to me. God, I feel like a bitch for questioning any of this.

"Might find out what?"

"Nothing," I say. "All I know is that daddy left everything to him. Why? I don't know. I can't even begin to understand the reasons why."

"Maybe your father just wasn't in the right mental state as he got closer to death," Nat suggests. "And since Liam was the only one around, he gave him everything."

"Wouldn't that mean Liam took advantage of him, though? If he knew my father wasn't right in the head, he shouldn't have accepted anything from him." This train of thought makes me uncomfortable.

"Hmm... possibly," Nat says slowly. "Then again, you can't be sure what happened." Nat pauses as if something occurs to her. "But if you had these concerns all this time, why did you go that far with him?"

Her words make me sick to my stomach. I feel cheap all of a sudden. "You're right, Nat," I say weakly. "I had no business going that far with him, and yet I did. I feel like such a whore for putting out on the first day."

"Please," Nat snorts, and I can practically hear her roll her eyes. "I don't know any whores who get paid to get eaten out. And if you aren't happy with that, I'd be overjoyed to take your place."

"Oh Nat," I say and laugh. "Leave it to you to say something like that."

"Seriously, Lizzie, you're overthinking this way too much. Do you really like this guy?"

"I do... well, at least I think I do."

"Hmm. Well let me ask you this--do you like the way he makes you feel?"

I think about the sweet side of Liam, how much of a gentleman he was on our date. How fun he was, back at his place. "Yes," I say finally. "I really do. He makes me feel... good."

"Okay then. Just have fun with it. No matter what happens. Just have fun."

The way Nat says it makes it seem so easy.

Maybe it is that easy, I think. *If I just give it a chance. Besides, I have time. I don't have to leave here to go back to school for almost two months.*

But what would happen after those two months? I feel a twinge of pain in my heart at the thought of leaving.

After a second, I push those thoughts away. I need to stop worrying and just let things happen. It's not like I'm in a committed relationship with Liam. For all I know, we're not meant to be anything more than fuckbuddies.

Maybe he's just in my life to provide me with a distraction to my grief, and that's it.

"What harm can it do?" Nat presses. "It's just a little fun."

I decide I'm going to heed Nat's advice. After all, what harm could it do?

I smile and finally reply, "I can do fun."

Chapter 11

Liam

"Where were you last night?" Zac's on me as soon as I walk in the office.

I sigh heavily and walk right past him, answering, "What's it matter?" I went out and saw my Elle last night. Just a movie date. No sex, nothing. Just the two of us cuddling on the sofa and watching *Up*. It's a stupid kids' movie. But she picked it out. She said it was sweet. She cried in the beginning a little, and I wondered why she'd pick something that would do that to her, knowing how the beginning starts. But I think I know why. And it made me happy to hold her and be there for her.

I'm really starting to like this broad. A week later, and I'm still interested in just being around her. It's different for me.

But then again, recently a lot of things have been different. Starting with her old man.

"You're just gonna keep running back to the 'burbs to get laid, is that it?" Zac asks me with contempt. I don't like the way he's talking. I give him a hard look and he settles down a bit.

"What the fuck is up your ass?" I snap back at him as I take a seat in my chair.

"We got a threat last night." My jaw clenches. I fucking hate some of the assholes we do business with. I look up at my brother and wait for more.

"From Ian?" I ask him. He wouldn't be the first. It's common for guys who place bets they can't afford to threaten us later, rather than pay up. It doesn't happen often, but it does happen. It's useless for them to do it. We always have collateral, and we always get paid. We'd be stupid to take a bet that can't be repaid. That's why we look into our clients. So those threats get muted pretty fucking fast.

But for Zac to be this pissed and this worked up, it's gotta be Ian's doing. He nods his head, confirming it. I run my hands through my hair. Fucking hell. My first thought is that I don't wanna deal with this shit. I'd rather be back with Elle, holding on to her and kissing up her neck. I might be warming up to her, but she's heating up for me, too.

Zac clears his throat and gets my attention again.

"Why the fuck is he bothering us now?" This fucking asshole needs to get out of our business. I'm done with him.

He's a fucking nobody.

"He didn't like that we were giving him a bad name."

"What's that supposed to mean? His name doesn't come out of our mouths."

"A couple of the guys were pissed they had to pay up front and asked why," he replies.

I give my brother a hard glare. "And what'd you tell them?"

"It wasn't me," he answers defensively.

"Fucking Tyler." Why's there always gotta be something? "We shoulda just cut those clients."

"Some of the high rollers come from Ian, too."

"Yeah," I say and let the anger slip away easily; my brother's got a point, and there's no point in thinking that way. "What's the threat?"

"That he's gonna 'gut us like the fucking pigs we are and bleed us out'."

"What a fucking prick." The threat doesn't even faze me. I've heard worse from more capable people.

Zac pulls out his phone and shows me a video of fat fuck named Gino Stalone shoving a note into the mailbox we have around back. I recognize him. He's one of the assholes that tried to work me over when they first heard about us. He's still walking with a limp because of me. He should've done a better job. Instead he came at me with a punch and took a bullet to the kneecap for his troubles.

"You know that saying, don't shoot the messenger?" Zac

asks me.

I grin at him as he adds, "I told Tyler it was a shit saying."

"So he's taking care of it?" I ask Zac, just to make sure we're on the same page.

"Yeah, Ian should get the message loud and clear tonight." I don't like that it's coming to violence. But some things are only resolved this way.

"Good." I sit back in my chair, but I'm tense knowing a war is coming. I'm not backing down. My eyes fall to my desk and I see a manila envelope. My heart races in my chest with a hint of anger.

"What the fuck is this?" I ask.

Zac looks at it with a frown and then recognition crosses his face. "It came from some lawyer. He said you were expecting it."

I nod my head and try to calm the fuck down. Not everything is a threat. It's a note from Richard. When I called to tell the lawyer to do whatever paperwork had to be done to transfer it all to Elle he told me about it. I left the reading before he could give it to me.

I slowly pick up the envelope and consider opening it. I see Zac stand from the corner of my eye.

"We good?" he asks.

"Yeah, it's all good." He watches me for a moment and then glances to the envelope. "He said it was from that old man."

"Yeah," I say, and my chest tightens with pain. We don't

show emotion much. Well, except for anger. That's one we see a lot. But for him to be checking on me like this, it's unusual.

"It's all good," I repeat, and my brother nods and makes his way to the door.

Before closing it he asks, "Is she good, too?" It catches me off guard. A part of me relaxes though. I like that he's asking about her.

I stare him in the eyes for a moment, considering what he's asking. "She's doing okay. She's working through it." It's gonna take time for sure. But she's doing good I think.

He nods his head and looks at the floor before taking in a deep breath. "If you need anything, let me know." With that, he leaves.

I'm lucky to have my brother. Poor Elle doesn't even have that. I don't know how I survived my father's death, but it definitely had something to do with the people who surrounded me. And she has no one. Except me. And I'm basically using her for my own selfish needs.

I feel like a fucking asshole for thinking it, but it's true. I'm using that poor girl to make myself feel better. I throw the envelope down on the desk and cover my face with my hands. I'm a fucking bastard for it. She's clinging to me to help her get over her father's death. And I'm just counting the days until I can get her underneath of me. I'm such a fucking prick.

She's a good girl; she didn't even wanna fuck. She has morals and virtue. And here I am sifting through fucking threats and making sure pricks get what they deserve.

I've been working my ass off to make the operation legit and avoid this kind of shit, but it keeps coming back to me.

The image of Gino or Ian or any of those assholes coming up to me while I'm with her, or shit even while I'm next door to her, makes my blood boil. I'll kill them all before they touch her.

My heart beats faster, and my gut twists with pain. I should leave her now, before anything gets out of hand. Who am I kidding though, it's already out of hand. If they knew about her... my throat closes with worry. I know they're going to come after us. I can't give them an easy target. I can't let her get caught up in this shit.

I know I should end it with her today. I'm not good enough for her. I never will be.

I *need* to let her go. She's doing better. She'll be fine without me. Fuck, I don't want to. I haven't wanted anything in so long. I run my hands in my hair, not knowing what I should do. I'd be a selfish prick to keep her.

I already know that. I never should have chased her. My heart clenches in my chest. She's got a life, she's got schooling to go back to so she can have a real career. She'll be alright without me. She'll be *better* without me.

I've been living in a fantasy world with her, and this is my reality. I need to wake the fuck up before I get her hurt. Or worse.

I look down at the envelope on the desk. Maybe Richard

left it all to me so we could meet. Or maybe he thought he truly owed it to me. I snort and refuse to look at it.

The reason doesn't matter. He was a fucking asshole for doing that. For teasing me with a woman I never stood a chance at being good enough for.

I take a deep breath and pick up my phone. I do the right thing before I can stop myself. I type in the message and send it. It fucking shreds me.

Chapter 12

Lizzie

I'm sorry. It's over - L.

I stare at the text blankly, feeling a lump form in my throat. The words repeat over and over in my mind as I sit on the couch. *It's over.* I shake my head. I can't wrap my mind around this. Didn't Liam claim that he wanted to get to know the real me? And now he's breaking it off? I thought everything was going great. Like better than great. It was perfect. I thought we were perfect together. I feel blindsided. I didn't have a clue that he felt differently.

I tear my eyes away from the text, anger threatening to overwhelm me.

He's breaking up with me because he's mad I didn't have sex with him.

Or maybe it was because I still haven't gotten him off? In a way, I feel bad that I didn't. He made me feel incredible. Gave me a mind-blowing orgasm. I actually feel guilty over it, which is bullshit considering how I offered to... take care of it. But that was over a week ago!

And now he's breaking up with me. Fucking asshole.

There's no use going over the shoulda coulda wouldas, I think to myself. *If Liam really cared about me and wanted to get to know me like he claims, he wouldn't break up with me over something so trivial. He said he'd be there when I was ready. More bullshit.*

The more I think about this, the angrier I get. He had no right to do this. Come into my life. Get me addicted to him... and then just leave.

Fuck this! I rage. *I'm going over there right now to give that bastard a piece of my mind.*

I've been thinking about it all day. I know he's there. His shiny car is right there in the fucking driveway, taunting me.

You know what? I'm doing it. What do I have to lose? Nothing. Nothing to fucking lose.

I march outside and walk next door. Instead of using the doorbell, I ball a fist and pound on the door as hard as I can. It hurts my knuckles, and the cold weather doesn't help. It's only then that I realize I'm in my thin nightgown and it's freezing out here.

As the realization hits me, Liam yanks open the door.

My breath leaves my lungs at the sight of him. He has no shirt on, his chiseled abs proudly on display, and he's only wearing a pair of basketball shorts. Shorts that show off his huge cock imprint. I whip my eyes back up to his and ignore my need to look back down.

At first Liam looks shocked, and then hurt. He's quick to cover it with anger though. "Didn't I tell you last time that there was a doorbell?" he growls.

I haughtily reply, "I didn't feel like using it."

Liam responds with a tight voice. "I can see that." Why is he so pissed? He has no right to be pissed.

"It's over?" I demand. "It's over?"

Liam doesn't reply and just looks at me stoically. God, it fucking hurts. It feels like my heart is just splitting in two. Am I really that big of a fool?

I do my best to hold back the tears that threaten to spill from my eyes. "Hello?" I persist. I hate how my voice is about to crack. How I feel like bursting in tears and collapsing in his arms.

Liam scowls, making me feel even worse. "Look, what do you want from me?" he growls. "You got your fucking house. You should be happy to be rid of me. After all, I'm a fucking dirtbag asshole."

"That's not true--"

"Those words came from you," he says.

It hurts because I did say that, but I apologized and it was so long ago. At least it feels like it was long ago. "I called you those names in a moment of weakness." I try to defend myself, but he just crosses his arms in front of him. His entire stance is aggressive and standoffish, but his eyes are pained. I don't know what I did. I don't know how to fix this. I didn't mean it when I called him that. He has to know that.

"I'm sorry." He just stands there still, waiting for me to leave.

"Is that why you don't want me?" I practically whisper. My anger is nonexistent now. Instead I'm just heartbroken.

His hard features soften, and he looks apologetic for a moment. He takes in a deep breath and says, "I'm not good for you. You already know that. You don't want me." He shakes his head slightly and looks at me with sympathy. It only makes me angrier.

"I can decide what I want for myself!" My body starts to shiver, and I look back to my house and then past him into his living room. It's so fucking cold.

"Go home, Elizabeth."

He begins to shut the door, but I wedge my foot into the opening before he can close it. I'm lucky he didn't slam it. I would've lost my whole fucking foot.

"If you wanted me to suck your dick, then you should've just let me!" I scream at him out of anger.

"Do you think that's what this is about?" he asks me, and

suddenly I feel sick. My cheeks burn with embarrassment and my heart clenches in my chest.

He takes a step closer. "You think I don't want you 'cause you didn't suck me off?" He looks at me incredulously.

"I wanted to! I wanted to fuck you, too! I was just scared!" After screaming at him and taking several deep breaths, I finally register what he asked. "It has to be that," I insist. He doesn't respond, he just looks back at me with a look of disbelief. "I can't think of any other reason..." My voice trails off. God, I feel like an idiot. My insecurities run rampant.

"You deserve better than me." He tries to back away again, and it pisses me off. The whole 'it's me, not you' routine? Yeah, whatever. He can shove that excuse up his ass.

"You're not running away from me that easy!" I snap. "You're going to tell me what's wrong or so help me God--"

"Or what?" Liam says with a menacing threat. "What are you going to do about it?"

Anger swells within my chest. I grasp at that anger for dear life. I'd rather feel that than the hollowness of being dumped. What have I done to deserve this treatment? Liam can't treat me this way. I won't let him.

Unthinkingly, I lash out, slapping Liam across the face as hard as I can. His head whips to the side. Damn. That felt good. It's like déjà vu, only this time, it's warranted.

Liam slowly turns his head back to face me. There's a red mark where I've struck him. And anger. Incredible anger in his eyes.

"You don't think I want you?" He grabs my hips and brings me inside his house, slamming the door closed. "Oh, I fucking want you."

Growling with anger, he grabs me and slings me up against the wall. He presses his hard body into me, letting me feel how hard his big cock is. "You want me, Elizabeth?" he grunts. "You sure this is what you want?"

"If you want me, then fucking take me!" I scream at him.

"You're about to get fucked, Elle. If that's something you don't want, now would be the time to say something."

"I told you I want you--" Before I can finish, Liam's lips are pressed against mine. I instantly part my lips and deepen the kiss. His hot tongue mingles with mine as his hands travel down my body.

He pushes up my nightgown, and then pulls my panties off of me, exposing my swollen pussy. My clit throbs, and I push my pussy against his hand.

"Fuck, Elle. You're dripping wet for me." He breathes out the words as if I'm torturing him.

I look into his eyes and tell him again. "I want you, Liam." I do. I want him so fucking bad. I need his touch. I need him. Can't he tell?

The word *please* is on the tip of my tongue, but he jams his fingers inside of me, probing, thrusting before I can get it out.

Oh fuck, he feels so good. The heels of my feet dig into

his ass, pushing him closer to me as he fingerfucks me.

I groan and arch my back against the wall. Yes! My nipples harden and the sadness of him pushing me aside before diminishes as the pleasure burns low in my belly.

"I want you," he whispers in the crook of my neck as his fingers stroke my G-spot, bringing me closer and closer to my orgasm. He kisses my neck, my jaw, and then my lips. All the while pleasuring me. Yes!

He breaks our kiss and looks at me with heat in his eyes. "You have no idea how much I fucking want you." His confession confuses me, but I don't have the energy to think about it. There's one easy answer that's begging to spill from my lips.

"Then take me," I moan out and then gasp as he removes his fingers, leaving my throbbing pussy unsatisfied.

The high I felt as I approached the edge of my release vanishes as he backs away from me.

I blink several times, not understanding why he pulled away and then glare at him. I swear to God if he's leaving me high and dry like this it'll be the cruelest thing anyone has ever done to me.

"How much do you want me?" Liam asks in a husky voice as he shoves down his shorts and strokes himself.

My mouth waters and I lick my lips as a bead of precum forms on the seam of his head. If that's what he wants, fine. I want him. Even more, I want him to know how much I need his touch. I have no shame in giving him the pleasure he gave me.

I try to get down on my knees, but he stops me, grabbing my wrist. I see hesitation in his eyes as he searches my face. "I told you, you don't have to do that."

"But I want to," I whisper. He takes a step forward and grabs my ass in his hands, picking me up and pushing my back against the wall.

"This is how I want you," he says, looking deep into my eyes. My heart races in my chest. He lines his dick up as his lips crash against mine with desperation. In one quick thrust, he's buried deep inside of me and I scream out with pleasure.

My body heats as he slowly pulls out and then hammers his hard cock into me. His large girth stretches my walls, but he doesn't give me a moment to adjust. My breathing halts, and my head thrashes. My nails dig into his shoulders. I want him closer and deeper, but I also need him farther away. It's too intense. It's too much. But it feels so fucking good.

"I fucking want you," he growls as he picks up his pace. My back pounds against the wall with his merciless pace. A strangled cry is ripped from my throat.

I scream out his name as he ruts between my legs, kissing and biting my neck.

My nails scratch along his bare back as I try to escape the intense pleasure, but he has me pinned. My chest heaves, and my head slams against the wall as an overwhelming pleasure paralyzes my body. My toes stick out straight and I fall recklessly over the edge. My mouth opens with a silent scream as my body tenses and then my nerve endings come alive all at once, exploding with indescribable pleasure, and I find myself screaming out his name.

He groans my name in my ear and thrusts short shallow strokes, each one rubbing against my throbbing clit and prolonging my orgasm. My nails dig into his back and my teeth press down on his shoulder as my pussy clamps down on his dick and waves upon waves of pleasure rock through my body.

I sag against him, catching my breath, and he holds me for a moment before setting me down on the floor. I feel so weak. My entire body is limp and heavy.

I lean panting against the wall as Liam pulls his shorts up and heads down the short hallway to the kitchen. My pussy is sore, and my clit is still throbbing. I close my eyes and rest my hot cheek against the cool wall and try to calm my racing heart.

I pick my panties up and pull them into place. There's a bit of cum on my thigh, but I try to ignore it.

The lust-filled haze quickly dissipates and I look down the hall and to the door as Liam turns on the faucet.

How pathetic am I? I wrap my arms around my shoulders. He dumped me, and I came over here and let him fuck me. My mouth opens as I realize that's exactly what happened. I cover my face and try to keep myself from crying.

I should just leave before he has a chance to kick me out and give me another it's-not-you-it's-me speech.

Before I can make my move, I hear Liam's hard steps come

down the hall. The old wooden floor creaks and he comes back into the foyer with a neatly folded, damp paper towel.

He stops in his tracks as he registers the look on my face. I keep my eyes on the floor. I can't believe how pathetic I am.

"I'm gonna go," I manage to say and take a step toward the door. He reaches out and grabs my waist, stopping me and forcing me to look up at him.

His mouth opens, but he doesn't say anything for a moment. My heart barely beats in my chest. Finally he says, "I have some cocoa," he nods to the kitchen, "if you wanna stay."

I look back at him, not knowing what to say. I only want to stay if he really wants me to. If he really wants me.

As if reading my mind, he takes my hips in his hands, pulling me closer and puts his nose against mine. "I'm sorry." He kisses the tip of my nose and I close my eyes. "I'm sorry I texted you that. I want you, Elle." He brushes the hair out of my face and adds, "Please stay with me tonight." He kisses my hair. "I don't want you to leave."

Chapter 13

Liam

So much for ending it. I look over my shoulder at my Elle. I tried to do the right thing. That's gotta count for something. She should've walked away. Now she's mine. She has no fucking clue what she's gotten herself into. I don't give a shit though. I'm not letting her go now.

Elle takes a deep breath as we sit on the sofa. She's got her mug in both her hands and she brings it up to her chin and blows. She's not looking at me. I know she's still feeling a certain way about me doing that shit. I made her dinner, and we ate in mostly comfortable silence with my arm wrapped around her waist. I don't mind eating with my left hand if that means I can give her some of the comfort she needs. But she's still not quite right. It'll take time, but she'll forgive me for being an ass. I know she will.

"You okay?" I ask as I wrap my arm around her hips and bring her a little closer. I'm careful not to tug her too hard so her cocoa doesn't spill.

She looks up at me with her beautiful eyes and it breaks my heart. "I don't know that I'm going to be okay."

I lean forward and set my cup down on the coffee table. She will be, I'll make sure she will. "I said I'm sorry." I put a hand on her thigh and keep eye contact with her. I wish she'd put her cup down, but she's holding on to it for dear life.

She shakes her head gently and her long dark hair shifts slightly. "I mean..." She clears her throat and puts the cup down before lifting her feet onto the sofa and hugging her knees. I let my hand fall to the sofa. She doesn't look at me. "About my dad."

Her eyes go glassy and I don't know what I should do. That's something I just can't make right. She needs time for that.

"I'm sorry." I kiss her hair and pull her into my lap, shifting my weight on the sofa and leaning back. Thankfully, she leans into me. I gently run my hand up and down her arm. "He loved you so much." I remember how he showed me her picture for the first time. He was so fucking proud.

It was the morning after I spent my first night in this place. I'd walked in with a bottle of scotch, thinking about my own father. I threw the key onto the counter and looked around the place. My old house kinda looked like it. But this place was almost completely empty. All that was here was the old kitchen set, joined by me and the scotch. And memories of my mother and father. Mostly of my dad, lying in that fucking hospital bed. I remember the beeping of the machines, and the lines on the screen that meant he was still alive.

I drank a bit too much and passed out in the living room. I don't even know why I went to his house. I made up some lame excuse. Hungover and looking like shit, he let me in though. First thing he did after making a pot of coffee was show me her picture.

"Why..." She starts to ask something, but then shakes her head and reaches for the cup.

"Why what?" I ask her. I don't care what her question is; at this point, I'll break the damn vow I made to him. She needs closure. And if I can give it to her, I will. "Why did he leave everything to you?" she asks and her voice croaks.

She's quick to add, "It's not about the money. It's not that, it's just..." She pushes away from me and grabs the cup again. She doesn't drink it though, she just takes in a breath and stares straight ahead.

"I know, I know." I pet her back, helping to calm her a little. "You wanna know if you did something wrong. And you didn't. I know you didn't. He..." I trail off, remembering the note on my desk at the office. I wish I'd read it. Maybe he would've made some fucking sense in it. "I don't know why.

Maybe he felt like he owed me. He didn't though."

She looks at me for a long moment. "Did you know?" she asks. "Did you know he was dying when you met him?"

I can't lie to her. "Yeah. I knew."

She nearly spills the cup. I take it from her and set it down. "How long?" she asks in a voice cracked with sadness as tears run down her face. "How long did he know?"

"A while," I answer her. I can see her heart breaking right in front of me. "Twelve weeks."

Her shoulders shake with a loud sob and she covers her face with her hands, trying to climb farther into my lap. Like she can't get close enough to me.

"He told you, but not me!" she cries into my chest.

I kiss her hair and shush her. "He didn't want you to see him like that. He was hoping the treatments would work."

She takes in a ragged breath and says, "But I talked to him." Her words are forced, and I can barely make them out. "He could have told me. I wish I'd been there. I would've wanted to be there with him!"

No she doesn't. She doesn't know what it was like those last few days. I hired the nurses to do all that shit, but in the last week and a half, he could barely move. I know what she means, and I still wish he'd given her that choice.

"He just wanted what was best for you." I hold her for a while longer, while she cries it out of her system. After a while she looks up at me, pulling away from my embrace.

Her face is red and her cheeks are tearstained. Somehow she looks even more beautiful.

"But why you?" she asks.

"I don't know." I answer her with the truth. "I offered him help. And he accepted."

She takes a few minutes to calm herself down.

"I could've helped him," she whispers. Her eyes close, but she doesn't cry. She reaches for the cocoa and takes a small, cautious sip. "I wish I'd been there for him."

"You were with him. Every day he told me stories about you."

She looks back at me with vulnerability. "Can you tell me?" she asks weakly.

"Tell you the stories?"

"Please," she whispers. I lean forward and take her lips with my own. My heart hurts so much for her.

When I pull away and look down at her, her eyes are still closed and she's leaning into my touch. I rub my thumb along the bare skin of her thigh. I wish I could take all that pain away.

"Of course," I say and tell her every damn story I can remember.

I hold her small body and start with the first one he told me. It's easy to remember that one. And I just keep going. Some of them make her laugh, and a lot of them make her cry. But she lets me hold her the entire time, and just telling her what she meant to him makes the weight lift off my chest.

When I finish the last story and look down at her, she's passed out. Her chest rises and falls with steady breathing and I easily pick her small frame up and carry her to bed.

I hold her close to me while I try to fall asleep, but it's not till she rolls over and grips onto me, resting her face against my chest, that I'm able to drift off into a deep sleep with her.

Chapter 14

Lizzie

I *don't know what I should do,* I think to myself as I sit down at my computer desk in my bedroom. I haven't checked my school email in days, and I intend to play catch up. But I can't. I keep thinking about Liam.

There's also the dilemma that I have yet to receive any money, and I feel like a whore for even thinking about bringing it up.

One date. He hands over my inheritance. That was the deal, and he told me he talked to the lawyer.

It bugs the shit out of me. I don't know why. I need the money. I have to pay this upcoming semester's tuition, but I don't want to bring it up. I'm so uncomfortable about the entire thing. I love it when I'm with him. I can escape from all this shit. But then when he leaves I have to face the real world. And that world needs money.

Fuck! I don't want to bring it up. I really can't stand the fact that I'm going to have to ask him if he's sending it over soon. It's so awkward.

I have the urge to call Nat and tell her about my problem. At the same time, I don't want to talk to her. She's already told me to relax and to just have fun. I'm going to make myself look insane if I call her back, crying about how wishy-washy I'm feeling. I already know what I'm feeling for him this early is just crazy.

Nevermind looking cray cray, I think to myself. *I'll look more like a whore.* Shit. Thinking about it makes me feel absolutely shitty. But as the saying goes, the truth hurts.

Trying to push my gloomy thoughts away, I log into my email and go through all the unread messages. Then I go about checking my schedule for next semester and looking to see what textbooks I need to order.

I figure if this thing with Liam crashes, I'll be able to return to school and bury myself in my studies. Except I can't even think straight. I'm so damn conflicted. About everything.

Relax, I tell myself. *Breathe.*

I practice a meditation exercise, trying to ease the stress in my body with deep breathing. It doesn't work. Sighing in frustration, I blow the hair out of my eyes and look around the room. I hate this. I hate being here. This big, fucking empty house.

Tears pool in my eyes and I get angry. God damn it! I'm so fucking tired of crying!

I shouldn't be here. I should've gone back already. I need to ask Liam for my money and just leave. That's what I should do. What I feel for him is unhealthy and probably only because of my grief. I don't need a professional to tell me that. It's too soon and too fast.

I don't need him. I don't care how he makes me feel. A couple of months after I'm gone, I won't even remember his name. He's just a crutch. Someone to distract me from my pain. I can survive without him.

Pain stabs me in the chest. I don't know if it's from the thought of leaving Liam, or from the reminder of daddy.

I need to get out of this house, I think to myself. *Do something other than wallow in misery. Like fuck Liam.*

It's horrible. I know it's wrong to be thinking about sex with a man I'm so conflicted by. I just can't help it.

I jump up from my desk and grab my coat. I need to get out of this house. Some time to think, and then I'll decide. I either make a commitment to Liam and get one in return, or I leave him. I can't use him, and I can't let him use me.

And that's exactly what we're doing.

Chapter 15

Liam

I'm gonna fuck this up. Every day I'm waiting for her to tell me she's pissed about something. I fucking love what we have, but I know I'm gonna ruin it. I've never done this before and I'm not the kind of man who knows how to hold onto a woman. I've never tried to, and I don't wanna put myself out there when they can leave me. That's what people do, they leave you. I don't want that. But for her, I feel like I don't have a choice. Everything in me wants to be with her. And I'm just waiting for the moment she ups and leaves me.

And it's 'cause of Richard. The reminder of him brings me to the desk in the living room. It's an old flimsy desk, nothing like what I have at work. Richard had asked me to store it here while he was sorting through his things, making preparations for the end. But on top of it is that damn note. I brought it home from the office and I still haven't read it.

I sit down and stare at it. It's just a piece of paper. It's fucking harmless, but it's making my heart beat faster than it should. I take a deep breath and try to calm myself. Why am I being such a little bitch about this?

What if there's something in it for her? That thought has me reaching out and opening the letter. I don't know what his last words to me are, but if they're something she needs, I need to know right now.

The sound of the paper unfolding and soft crinkles as I hold it are the only things I can hear other than the blood rushing in my ears and the thud of my own heartbeat. I shouldn't have worked this up so much in my head, but I have.

Dearest Liam,

Well, the time has come to say goodbye, but I wanted to tell you a few things that I found hard to say in person.

You remind me of myself. I never told you, but my father passed when I was young. I didn't take it very well.

If it wasn't for Elizabeth's mother, I never would have loved in my entire life. I was filled with anger and hate. But worse than that, I just didn't want companionship. I wanted to be alone.

Her mother forced her way in. But it was so much later in

life, and she passed away only years after having Elizabeth. I wish I'd met her sooner. I wish I'd had more time with her.

I made a mistake, Liam. I need you to fix it. I know you've done so much for me, but there's one last thing.

I regret it all. You were right. I wish I'd spent my dying days with her. It would have been selfish, because I know it would have hurt her to watch me die. Maybe that makes me an asshole, because I know how hard this was for you. But she isn't going to take this easy. And I can't stand the thought that she's going to live her life with pain and hate.

I need you to help her. I didn't teach her how to want companionship. I don't want her to live the way I did. I need you there for her.

I'm leaving everything to you. This will help. You'll need all the help you can get. Without something to hang over her head, you'll never get through to her.

If she wants to pound her fists on your chest, please let her.

I can see hurt in you, the same pain I had. Let her heal you, too. You're a good man, and I want her to have a man like you in her life.

I don't want you two to live the life I had. You deserve more. You deserve better.

I hope you'll find that in each other.

Best wishes and blessings for you two,
Richard

I stare at the note for a long time. I try to ignore the way my eyes are glassed over and the way my chest feels like something's wrapped around it, squeezing the air from my lungs.

I finally stand up and let my instincts take over. And they're telling me to go to her. To get lost in her touch. I pick up the phone and dial her number before taking a look outside. The phone rings and rings, but she doesn't answer. Her car's out front. I get her voicemail and decide to wait a minute. Maybe she's busy.

I run my hands through my hair, but all I can think about is that fucking note. I can practically hear him saying those words. My heart clenches, and I grip the cell phone tighter before calling her again. No answer.

I fucking need her right now. I shove shoes on my feet and swing the door open. I don't bother with a coat.

I need to feel her. I need to kiss her. I need her just as much as she needs me.

Chapter 16

Lizzie

I have my nose buried in a book when there's a knock at the door. I stop reading the dark romance, something I've been preoccupying my mind with to keep it off Liam, and get up from the couch. As I walk across the room, I don't even have to guess who's there.

Liam.

My heart begins to pound at the thought of seeing him. And I take a second debating on whether I should open the door, or ignore him for as long as I can.

Relax, I tell myself. *You can do this. I need to have this talk with him. This needs to stop now.*

Still, it takes me several deep breaths to get my pulse to

stop racing and for my anxiety to ebb.

A frigid blast of air hits me as soon as I open the door, and I shiver. My mouth goes dry when I see Liam standing there, silhouetted by a sea of white. He's dressed casually, as if it isn't below twenty degrees weather and snowing. He's just in jeans and a t-shirt.

Good God, I think to myself worriedly. *He's got to be freezing!*

"Liam, what are you doing out in the snow with no coat on? You could catch a cold," I say with concern.

"I'm fine," he replies. He walks past me without asking to come inside.

Anxiety washes over me as I close the door and turn to face him.

Shit. He's looking at me with that intense gaze of his. Trouble is brewing. I don't know if I can do this.

"I've been calling you, but you haven't answered," he says, accusation in his voice.

Ugh. So here it goes. This is going to be rough. "I know. I've just been thinking," I respond slowly.

Anger flashes in his eyes. "Thinking about what?"

"Don't look at me like that," I say, getting angry. This is hard for me. "I think we should stop this."

He clenches his jaw. "You came to me, remember?"

"I'm sorry," is all I can manage. It's the only thing I can say. None of this would've happened if I didn't want it in the first place. I used him. I know that now. And I really do feel like shit about it.

Liam asks quietly, "Sorry for what, Elle?"

Unbidden, tears flow from my eyes and down my cheeks. "I can't do this, Liam," I choke out. "I'm so sorry." It's hard to breathe. It feels like my heart's being ripped out of my chest.

Liam walks over to me and grabs me by the arms, forcing me to look into his eyes. Fuck. It hurts to see the pain reflected there. "And why not? You wanted this as much as I did."

I can't respond. The lump in my throat is too big to swallow. Why does it hurt so fucking much?

Liam looks at me with disbelief. "You really don't wanna be with me? Is that it?"

The pain is crushing me. Any more, and I feel my heart will shatter. "I don't know," I croak, seconds away from sobbing like a baby.

Liam looks like he's been stabbed in the heart. It's a look I can hardly bear. Surprisingly, he's not giving up. "Well, I don't give a shit. I still want to be with you, Elle. No matter what you say." He looks away and I realize he's trying to keep from crying. "You healed a part of me that I didn't realize was broken." His voice is thick with emotion and it threatens to send me over the brink.

"Please!" I cry. *Please don't do this. Not here. Not now.*

"Please what?" Liam presses.

"I don't know," I sob, shaking my head. "I don't know

what I want from you."

Liam pulls me into his arms, holding me close. It feels so good to be enveloped by the warmth of his hard body. "Well, what do you feel? What do you feel in your heart for me? 'Cause I can damn sure feel something in mine for you. And I want to hold onto it."

His words are so powerful. It scares the shit out of me. "But--but it's so soon. We're both grieving...and this is just... it just isn't healthy!"

Liam snorts derisively. "Says who? Who can tell us what's healthy, and what isn't? All I know is I feel for you, Elizabeth Turner. And I don't want it to end."

I can't find the words to reply. I feel for Liam, too. Maybe too much. That's what frightens the fuck out of me. "I'm scared," I say, finally admitting the truth to him.

Liam bends down and kisses the tears on my jaw, then kisses me on the lips. I taste the salt on them. "It's okay to be scared. There's nothing wrong with that. You just have to believe that everything will be alright." He kisses me again and I melt into him. I'm breathless when he pulls away a moment later. "This doesn't have to be anything that you don't want it to be," he says huskily. "We're moving fast right now, but I don't see anything wrong with it. I just need you to stop thinking about tomorrow, and only think about what's here and now."

He's asking a lot from me when I'm so conflicted. So

confused. I don't know what I should do. I don't know anything. "I don't know, Liam."

He kisses me again and I feel my defenses crumbling. "Please don't deny me, Elle. I want you." He injects even more feeling into his voice and says, "I need you."

At those words, and the pleading look in his eyes, my defenses are swept away like a leaf in a hurricane. I can no longer deny this man. I am his. Forever.

I melt into him and let him pull me into a strong, lingering kiss.

His lips crash against mine as he pushes me down on the ground and devours me. He pushes his hand up my shirt and lets his hands roam my body. He owns me, and he knows it.

His demanding touch sends shivers over every inch of me. I have to pull away and breathe in the hot air between us. He continues kissing along every inch of my neck with a desperate need.

"Liam," I whimper as he pushes my pants down and cups my pussy.

"Yes!" he says before nipping my earlobe. "I want you screaming my name," he harshly whispers. His words harden my nipples and spike my libido. He pulls my panties down as I take in uneven breaths.

I feel like I'm suffocating. Everything's going so fast. He pulls my shirt over my head and instantly kneads and sucks on my breasts. I'm caged under him. My senses are overwhelmed.

His smell. His touch. My body is on fire with desire.

He pushes his thick fingers into my wet pussy, and my back bows. My neck arches away from him as I scream out his name. "Mine," he whispers into my neck, continuing his torturous strokes. He doesn't let up as I try to move away from him. My body is tense and on edge. My release feels heightened and almost like too much as his thumb rubs against my throbbing clit in time with the pumps of his fingers stroking my G-spot.

"Cum for me," he commands and I obey. Every inch of my skin heats and ignites, and a wave of intense pleasure flows from deep in my belly outward in all directions. My body trembles, and my eyes close as Liam pushes my legs apart and settles between them.

He grabs my ass with both hands and tilts me up so he's in a better position. I can barely breathe, feeling as though I'm miles away.

My head thrashes wildly as he shoves himself deep into my pussy with one hard thrust. "Fuck!" I scream out.

Liam leans down and bites my shoulder, hard, as he pumps in and out of me.

"My name," he growls. He picks up his pace as he kisses the bite mark and grips my chin in his hand. I stare into his heated gaze as he continues to ruthlessly fuck me. My body jolts with each hard pump. "Scream my name."

My body heats as he stares into my eyes and continues

to pound into my pussy. I can barely breathe as the extreme pleasure intensifies. Each thrust bringing me closer to an edge that seems too steep.

My eyes start to close and I bite down on my bottom lip as the feeling becomes too much. Liam doesn't stop, he only pushes in deeper and harder. His pace gets faster and I lose myself to the overwhelming pleasure.

"Liam!" I scream out and he captures my voice with his lips on mine. He kisses me with a passion I've never felt. He devours my body as every limb feels heavy with a tingling pleasure. My pussy spasms around him as he thrusts deeper into me, making me grip onto his shoulders and scream into the crook of his neck.

His dick pulses, buried to the hilt and our combined cum leaks down my ass as my breath slowly comes back to me. He braces himself on top of me, whispering my name and leaving a trail of kisses down my neck and up my jaw. My chest rises and falls with deep, calming breaths of hot air. I push my hair out of my face and then take his face in my hands.

My heart swells and I start to tell him the words on the tip of my tongue, but he leans down and kisses me. Taking the words and silencing them.

I love you, Liam.

Chapter 17

Ian Dracho

I fucking hate that prick Liam Axton. He thinks he's so fucking smart. They're coming up with everything they can to destroy my business. Before him, I had it made. These hot shots come in here, thinking they know it all and how they're going to be walking out with their pockets full of my money. I snort a laugh. I'm the only one profiting in the deals I make.

Until Liam fucking Axton. My cell rings on the end table and I mute the game on the television. I need to know what Stephen found out there at Liam's new property. Gino's gone, and I know that fucker's the one who whacked him. I'm gonna make him pay. They'll all pay.

"What'd you find out there?" I answer the phone with the

one question that matters. What the fuck is Liam doing with a house out in the suburbs? It came up on his report, and I need to know why.

"Elizabeth Turner," Stephen says, followed by something muffled. He must be outside, judging by the wind blowing against his phone. I can hear the moment he gets back in his car and shuts the door. Everything's more clear. Except who the fuck Elizabeth Turner is.

"Who?" I lean against the back of my sofa and listen to Stephen a little more closely. He's supposed to be checking out the house, not talking about some cunt.

"He's at some broad's house next door."

"Liam is?" I ask. My forehead's pinched with confusion.

"Yeah, I just looked inside," he bellows a laugh. "Got me rock fucking hard."

"If this is just some chick next door that he's banging, I'm gonna be pissed." Something in me is telling me it's not though. Things have been off with that asshole recently. Now's the time to strike. He's weak. And it must be this bitch that's getting to him. "What the fuck is he doing with a house out there anyway?"

"Maybe it's for her?" Stephen sounds a little unsure, but I can't think of any other reason Liam Axton would be out in the suburbs. No fucking way he bought a house to get close to a woman. Unless she means something to him. A sick smile grows across my face.

“Stake it out and find out everything you can about this chick and what she means to him.” I wanna know everything. I wanna know how bad it’s gonna hurt him when I slit this bitch’s throat. I want him to see it. I’ll make this asshole pay. “If she’s valuable, then we’ve got a good way in.”

“You got it, boss.”

Chapter 18

Liam

I can still feel her kiss on my lips as I pull into the parking spot. My chest fills with warmth. It's a long ass drive from her place to work, but it's worth it just to wake up next to her. I've never had this before. It's still new and pure. I'm still afraid I'm going to ruin it, but so far she's happy. It's been almost a month since she's come back and shoved her way into my life. I don't know how I ever lived without her.

Every night we lay in bed and she falls asleep in my arms, I wonder if it's going to be the last night. If she'll wake up and realize she doesn't need me. But then I always wake up to her kissing my shoulder and nuzzling her head into the crook of my neck.

Life's never felt this good. I can't let it end. She's been talking about school and I know she's thinking about what's going to happen when she has to leave. I am too, but neither of us has said anything. We're both walking on eggshells, wondering how long this can possibly last. It's just too good to be true.

As I walk into the elevator a woman in a skimpy black dress gets on with me, looking more like a hooker than an employee of any of the businesses who rent out these spaces. I keep my eyes off her ass even as she bends over to select her floor. She looks back over her shoulder with a small smile as the doors close. She's looking at me like I'm a piece of meat.

A different time, I would've stopped the elevator and fucked her right here, right now.

Not now. Rather than feeling desire, I'm pissed. It's not her fault. She doesn't know I'm spoken for, but just the fact she's trying to do something that could cause friction between me and Elle makes me tense.

I give her a tight smile and her eyes fall as she straightens her shoulders and pulls her dress lower over her ass. Good. I feel a little bit like an asshole. But I'm glad the message was received.

I'm still feeling tense and off when I get to the top and walk into our space, although I don't know why.

Everything's pristine and in order. But it's quiet. No one's here. I clear my throat and try to get rid of this tension while I unlock my office.

I stop in my tracks as Zac turns in the seat across from my desk and stares at me. I look around the room. Tyler's not here.

"I don't want you to get upset," Zac says as I take deliberate steps to sit down at my desk. A million things are running through my head, but I have no real concrete idea as to what he's talking about.

"Spit it out," I tell him. I don't like not knowing shit. I don't like being tense and on edge, and that's exactly what I am right now.

He slides a photo across the desk. When he pulls his hand away, my blood chills. My heart stops working. It's just a photograph with a hole in the top. Maybe the size of a finishing nail from where it was hung on something.

It's a picture of us. Elle's smiling back at me. Her head's resting on my shoulder and she's looking up at me even though my eyes are on the television that's not in the picture. It's from one of our lazy nights together. In her house, and the picture was obviously taken from a window. Clearly someone's been watching us.

I pick up the photo gently. More carefully than I need to, but I'm afraid my anger is going to make me do something stupid. My entire body slowly heats as my blood fills with adrenaline.

"Tyler's keeping an eye on her now." Zac's words barely do a thing to calm me, but at least he's a step ahead of me.

"Where was it?" I ask Zac. I finally tear my eyes away from the picture. "In the mailbox like the last one?" I remember the threat from before, and my stomach wants to heave. Elle. I need to get to her.

"Yeah," he says easily, although it's completely at odds with how on edge he looks. He looks as though he's going to have to defend himself. He's waiting for me to attack him. But he's not my target. Maybe he's just waiting for me to lose it. Yeah, that's probably more accurate.

"You okay?" he asks. But I ignore him. I flip the picture over, looking for a message. But there's nothing there.

"Anything with it?" I ask him as my thumb rubs over the spot in the picture where her hand's in mine.

"No," he answers in a clear, low voice.

She's so fucking beautiful. That moment was for us. And now it's tainted. I have to put the picture down as my hands fist and I struggle to fight the urge to break everything around me in this fucking room. I need to hold back this rage.

But I also need to do something.

I'm quick to pick up my phone. Zac's eyes go wide and he shakes his head as he says, "That's what he wants, Liam." I ignore my brother's warning. I don't care if I'm giving Ian the reaction he wants.

The phone rings once, twice. *Pick up the phone, you fucking coward*. On the end of the third ring, the phone clicks and I hear his breathing on the end of the phone.

I stand quickly and make my way to the large window in the room. "Leave her out of this," I say simply in a dark voice

I don't even recognize.

"You fucked with me, now I fuck with you," Ian says and then the line goes dead.

My body's shaking with rage. She's mine. I finally got a life I want. A life I'm afraid is going to slip through my fingers. He's not going to take that away from me. He's not going to do a damn thing to her. I'll fucking kill him first.

My chest heaves with an angry breath as I look my brother in the eyes and say, "I want him dead."

Chapter 19

Lizzie

Crap, I think as I open the fridge and peer inside. *There's nothing to eat.* I have no idea why there's no food in there. Probably because I've been so focused on Liam and forgetting to do normal things, like go grocery shopping. The strange thing is, my appetite is starting to return. What I wouldn't do for some of Nat's delicious sugar cookies right now. Or chocolate. Or wine. Or better yet, all three. I need a real meal though.

My stomach growls as I close the fridge and take a look around the kitchen. It looks different now than it did when I came home. He didn't have half the things I use in the kitchen, so new things have been added to the counter. I threw away a few of the old things he'd kept. A couple I know were my mother's. Like her mixer. I'm keeping that. I'll never throw that away.

I think I'm getting better with dealing with the pain. I find myself no longer thinking of daddy a million times a day, or when I do, I don't instantly burst into tears. Even now, the picture of his face on the fridge only makes my heart hurt a little. I don't want to rip it down and sob inconsolably on the floor.

A feeling of guilt washes over me as I gaze at his portrait. I should still be grieving, shouldn't I? It hasn't even been that long since daddy died, and I'm already forgetting about him.

It just isn't right.

It's Liam, I think to myself. *He's filling that awful void left by daddy.*

If anything, this realization makes it worse. I'm already moving on with my life.

But isn't that what daddy would want? For me to be happy? And with a man he obviously put so much trust in?

I have to believe this, otherwise the guilt is going to eat me alive.

The sound of the front door opening tears me out of my musing. My mood instantly brightens. Liam's here.

"I'm in the kitchen!" I yell, stifling the other emotions and trying to remember what I was doing in the kitchen to begin with.

Oh yeah, movie night. We've been having these little date nights, and I really love them. It's like real life is suspended when I'm with him. I know I have to face reality again at some point, but I don't want to. I just want what we have together.

I'm ignoring all the other responsibilities for as long as I have to. At least I've paid my tuition. The money came through, and everything's taken care of. Liam started the paperwork the day we went on our date. So for days I was worrying over nothing. He says I worry too much and to just trust him. So I have, and I have to admit, life's easier just letting him take care of me. I don't really have any worries, other than my grief over my father passing. But it's getting better. It really is. With Liam helping me, I can keep inching my way toward normalcy.

I'm just trying to live in the moment with Liam and forget that this could be over soon when I have to go back to school. It's better that way. I pull my hair in front of one shoulder and smile thinking about our movie night tonight.

I haven't been to the theatre in so long. I can't wait to go. And have popcorn. I *must* have buttery movie popcorn. It's crazy how much I want it. Just a week ago the thought of having greasy popcorn would make me want to barf. Now I'm craving it like a junkie.

"Liam?" I ask when I hear no response. For a moment, I'm rattled. It's unusual for Liam not to respond. The sound of footsteps grows louder, and my anxiety increases. My heart starts to pound and all sorts of wild scenarios began running through my head when Liam appears in the doorway.

I breathe out a sigh of relief at the sight of him. "Oh thank God, it's you," I say breathlessly, my hand pressed over my heart. "For a moment there, I thought someone had broken in." His eyes flash with worry, but it's gone so quickly I think I just imagined it.

I pause and then add, "You ready to go see Warcraft?"

Instead of responding, Liam just nods. I immediately suspect something's off. My heart twists in my chest. Maybe he's not feeling the same way about me as I am about him. Maybe he's ready to talk about what's going to happen when I go back to school. Fuck, I'm not ready for that.

"Is something wrong?" I ask cautiously.

"Nah." He's lying. I know he is.

"You sure?"

"I'm fine," he replies curtly. Now I really know something is wrong. But I'm not quite sure what to do.

He holds up a DVD. "I wanna stay in tonight." My lips tip down into a frown. It's not that I don't want to stay in. I love it when we do, I was just looking forward to going out. And to getting that popcorn.

It's fine. I shake off all the weird insecurities running through me. Everything's fine. I'll feel better once we're cuddling up. Everything's better when he holds me.

"Well can we at least get some popcorn for the movie?" I ask, trying to change the subject. "I'm really craving some right now."

"We don't need it." My lips part, ready to protest. I can run right out to the convenience store and grab it in like twenty minutes. And I want it.

"But... I really would like to have some." I gesture at the fridge. "I'm hungry, and there's nothing to eat."

Liam sighs. "I don't want to go out, Elle."

Anger surges through me. What the hell is Liam's problem? I was really looking forward to going out and having a good time, and now he's pulling this.

My eyes fall and I struggle to keep my composure. It's gotta be my hormones and insecurities. I close my eyes and almost shake my head. I know it's something else. I can't keep lying to myself. If he's ready for this to end then he can just fucking do it.

Liam senses my anger because suddenly he's in front of me, pulling me into his arms. I use my hands to brace myself on his chest and I was right, just being in his arms soothes something in me.

I still feel vulnerable, until he kisses the tip of my nose. "I'm sorry, Elle," he apologizes. "I've just had a very long day." I close my eyes, letting his touch calm me. "If you really wanna go out, we will."

"Are we okay?" I whisper. I hate that I sound weak, but I can't help feeling like there's tension between us. I don't like it. I want it gone.

"Of course we are," he answers as I look up at him. There's

so much sincerity in his gaze that every insecurity vanishes. "I'm sorry, Elle. Of course we can get some popcorn for tonight."

I place a hand on his shoulder and gently rub it. "It's okay. You don't have to apologize. Since you're so worn out, do you want me to drive?"

He kisses me on the nose. "Nah. I'm fine. I'll drive. Where do you want to go?"

Chapter 20

Lizzie

I should tell her, but I can't do it.

She's gonna be pissed at me. She's going to know what kind of a bastard I am. She's going to question everything. Just knowing all that's going to happen tears me apart. I wanna keep this from her. I need to keep all this shit away from her.

I can't help but feel anxious as I drive down to the convenience store.

"Oh, shit!" My heart stills at Elle's outburst. "I forgot my purse." She sounds so upset. I close my eyes and try to contain my relief.

"No problem." I stop at a red light and dig in my back

pocket for my wallet. I have time to pull out a couple of twenties and pass them to her.

"I think one will do," she says in a soft voice. "Thank you," she says, a little uncomfortable. "I'll pay you back."

A smile cracks on my face for the first time since this morning. The light turns green and we move forward as I place my hand on her thigh. "No you won't. You're my girl." I pick her hand up and kiss her wrist, keeping my eyes on the road.

I hear her soft sigh and feel her eyes on me. I take a look from the corner of my eyes and she looks beautiful. It makes my heart hurt.

A small smile is playing on her lips. She's so perfect. I keep rubbing soothing circles as we drive up and I pull in. Right at the front doors, where there's plenty of security and high visibility. I can see everything. I've got my gun in the glove box. We should be fine, but it won't hurt to stay vigilant. I put the car in park and Elle's already moving. Her seat belt's off and she starts to open her door and holds up one finger.

"I'll be in and out real quick." She leans across the console and plants a kiss on my lips. "Promise." Her words echo in my ears as she opens her door.

My heart stops beating as I look past her. One of Ian's men pulls in, and even with his sunglasses on, I recognize him. Stephen.

It's freezing outside, but his window's down and I know why. He's going to shoot. It's a hit. My lungs refuse to fill.

My blood spikes with fear as everything plays in slow motion.

Before I can blink, he's pulling his gun out of the window and aiming it right at Elle. I grab her shoulders and pull her down. The bullets fly out with a loud *bang*! One ricochets off the car, I think the hood, and she screams. Another hits the passenger side mirror. She's still screaming, and her hands fly to her head. My heart's pounding in my chest.

"Stay down!" I yell at her, covering her with my body and struggling to close her door. Once I hear the click, I chance a look and peek up. *Bang*! He fires as I duck back down and she shrieks in fear.

Her window shatters as a bullet hits my driver seat. Small shards of glass fall into the car by her feet. She scoots closer to me and I try my damndest to cover her. This is too close.

I stay low. I just need to protect her. I reach up and unlatch the glove compartment to get my gun. I can feel it, but I fumble with it as my heart pounds. Finally, I've got it in my hand. The heavy weight does nothing to relieve my anxiety. She can't be here. I can't anything happen to her. The car's still running and I put it into reverse, desperate to get out of here. To get her on the other side of me.

Someone runs from the store and ducks behind a car. A few other people are screaming from inside the store as another wild spray of bullets hits the car. Elle's shrill cry pierces my ears as her fingers dig into my leg. She's staying down though and the door is closed. She's as safe as possible for now, but she could still get hit.

I only lift my head up enough to barely see that fucker and quickly shoot my gun, aiming right at his head. He ducks to avoid the first shot and then the second. I don't need to hit him. I just need to get him to stop firing so I can get her out of here. That's what matters. My heart races and my blood pumps with the fear of losing her.

I'm driving in reverse with one hand, my grip tight on the leather steering wheel. My other hand is still holding the gun while pushing down on her back, keeping her down. I hit the gas pedal and turn the wheel as sharp and fast as possible. The back of my car smacks against a lamppost, jolting our bodies. Elle screams again and tries to cover her head, curling into a small ball on the seat.

I put the car into drive and take off. The tires squeal as two more bullets hit the back of the car, each one making her jump and ripping a sob from her throat. She's shaking, and I'm doing everything I can to take care of her and get us out of here.

I look in my rearview expecting him to follow us, but he's turning out of the lot in the other direction. My heart's racing and she's clawing against my arm, trying to get out of my hold and sit up.

I release a breath I didn't know I was holding and let go of her. The light ahead turns yellow and I slam on the gas to get through the intersection. I'm not stopping. I'm taking her to my place in the city until these fuckers are dead. I don't trust going back to her place. I need my guns and my security system. I focus on my breathing; I need to get my shit together. She needs me, now more than ever. My heart's still racing like crazy, but it's starting to calm slightly.

"Oh my God." Tears fall down Elle's face. "Are you okay?" she screeches. Her breathing is frantic and she's looking around, the wind from her open window blows her hair into her face. The glass crunches beneath her feet as she moves slightly and then looks out of the back window like she's expecting to see him. She doesn't even know what she's looking for.

"It's okay, he's gone." I sound cold and devoid of emotion. But this is the most emotion I've ever felt. And it's not one I welcome. Fear. They almost took her from me.

"Did you see him?" Her wide eyes are filled with worry. "We need to call the cops." She searches the floor for her phone and picks it up. I'm quick to snatch it out of her hands, dropping the gun.

"No cops." My words are hard. But I can't let her do that. I'm killing these fuckers. As soon as I can get her safe, they're dead. They've been in hiding, but you can only hide so long. We know where they hang around and now we have their paper work, I know where they live and where their families live. I'm not giving them a chance to run. I'll find those fuckers. "They're all dead."

It's then that Elle sees the gun and puts two and two

together. Her eyes widen, and the fear in them changes. She's scared of *me* now. It makes my heart clench in my chest. It fucking hurts, but I knew this would happen. She pushes away from me and leans against the car door. Like she's desperate to get out.

"Why do you have a gun?" she asks; her voice is hollow. I press my lips into a firm line and stare straight ahead. "Why were they shooting at us?" Her voice cracks, and I can see she's shaking again.

"Elle--" I start to speak, but she screams out, "Tell me!"

"'Cause they have a hit out on me." I grip the wheel tighter and add, "On us." Her lips part with disbelief. It fucking hurts me to say that.

"Why?" she asks.

I take in a deep breath before looking at her and answering, "I told you I was a bad man."

"Stay away from me!" she screams. My heart shatters in my chest. I loosen my grip on the wheel and look out of the driver side window.

"That's not an option now." I finally tell her the truth, "I'm sorry, Elle. But you have to come with me."

Her mouth opens, and she struggles to breathe. I wish I could comfort her and that she'd believe me when I say I'll take care of this. But I can tell just from the look in her eyes, everything between us is broken.

Chapter 21

Liam

I open the car door for her and she storms out. She doesn't touch me; she completely avoids me. She's fucking pissed. Her arms are crossed, and she's not speaking. That's fine if she doesn't want to talk right now. I'll wait for her to calm down and figure out how to make this up to her. She's walking the wrong fucking direction though. And that's not going to happen. I'm not letting her leave.

"Elle, get your ass inside!" I yell out as I follow her down the driveway. We're a good distance away from the other houses, but they're within view, and I'm not letting her get close enough to them to cause a scene. My heart's trying to climb out of my throat. I need to get her ass inside. Right. Fucking. Now.

"Elizabeth!" I scream out her name.

She turns on her heels, the crunch of the gravel and my heartbeat the only sounds I can hear as she stares back at my house with anger. "I'm not going anywhere with you," she says with a shaky voice, finally looking at me. Her eyes are glassy. She's a mix of emotions and looks like she's ready to crack

"Elle," I say and put my hands up as though I'm approaching a wounded animal. That's what she is. I hurt her. I fucked up. I know I did. But I'm going to make this right.

She shakes her head and lets out a sarcastic laugh.

"Don't fucking call me that, and don't put your hands on me." She throws her finger out, pointing at me and looking at me with disgust. She walks backward down the driveway with every step I take to get closer to her. The ground's uneven, and I don't need her falling and hurting herself.

"I can't let you go, I'm sorry." I know she's pissed at me. But I'll be damned if I'm going to let her go. I have security here at least. It's something. And now that I know they're coming, she's not leaving my house until they're both dead.

"You can't make me stay here," she says with wide, unbelieving eyes. They're red and swollen from the threat of tears, but she's holding them back. She shakes with anger and sadness, and shouts, "I wanna go home!"

"You're in danger--"

"I can call the police--" she starts to say, cutting me off, but I nip that in the bud.

"No, you can't." I shake my head and take another step closer. She takes one back and her ankle nearly rolls as she kicks out the gravel under her feet. I need her to understand. I don't want to even say this shit out loud. But she needs to know how much danger she's in. "They'll come for you--"

"Because of you!" she shrieks at me, bending at her waist and practically spitting as she yells. I know it had to have hurt her throat. There are a few houses at the end of the drive and then nothing but the woods around the city park. I look over to see if anyone's there. She needs to knock this shit off.

"You need to get inside and stay there." She doesn't answer me. Her skin is bright pink from the freezing air. The wind's blowing harder now, and I know it's gotta be getting to her. Shit, I'm cold, too. "Come inside. And we can talk about this later."

Her eyes whip to mine. "Talk about this?" she asks incredulously, and raises her brows.

"I'll tell you everything you want to know. But right now, you need to go inside."

"What the fuck do you do?" she says and finally looks up at me. She waits for an answer, but I'm not ready to talk.

"You don't need to know right now." I don't want to get into this shit. I need to get her inside and take care of this problem.

She mutters under her breath, "I knew you were no good." It pisses me off to hear her say that. But mostly it fucking hurts.

"Yeah, I'm a real bad man," I admit, "but other bad men are after you."

"It's your fault," she says. And she's right.

"I'm sorry." I can't say anything else. She finally lets me take a step closer to her without moving away from me. "You just have to stay here until I deal with them."

"Kill them?" she asks hysterically.

"It's either you or them, Elle." Her breathing comes in pants, and she glances down the driveway like she's considering running and then looks back up to me.

She glares at me like she hates me. Like she regrets everything, and it makes my stomach churn.

"I trusted you," she says in a small voice.

"I promise I'll take care of you." She shivers and grips onto her arms, looking defeated but still closed off. I walk behind her as she concedes and slowly makes her way to the door.

"I don't want you to," she says with a coldness I've never heard from her. I swear my heart stops beating and sinks in my hollow chest.

"You don't have a choice."

Chapter 22

Lizzie

What have I gotten myself into?

I stare blankly up at the high ceilings, wondering how I'm going to get out of this mess. It doesn't seem real.

Liam's forced me to stay in his bedroom, a prisoner against my will. The bedroom is comfortable and all, beautiful actually, with a gorgeous view of the skyline and crown molding running along the walls painted a soft shade of cream, but it's still a prison nonetheless.

I shouldn't be here, I think to myself. *I don't belong here, or in this mess. How did I let it come to this?*

It's crazy how close I came to being killed. I was shot at! Never have I been in such fear for my life. Just remembering the bullets whizzing by causes me to hyperventilate. Out of nowhere, I become dizzy and the room begins to spin in front of my eyes. Then my heart starts racing so fast I think I'm having a heart attack.

Jesus, Lizzie, calm down!

It takes a few minutes of calm steady breaths, before I feel like I'm in control although I'm still shaking. After a moment, I sit up and notice I'm covered with sweat, my palms clammy.

I'm not okay. That is the only truth I know. I am not fucking okay.

I knew I never should've gotten involved with Liam, considering the murky details surrounding my inheritance. I should have just sued him and contested the will. No, I had to go fall for him when I should've known better.

Anger burns my cheeks. I'm so mad. Mad at myself.

I gave myself to him! I rage. *I let him eat me out on our first date.* I swallow back the fury in my throat. I feel so humiliated, cheap and worthless. *He so played me for a fool.*

Can my life be any more fucked? My daddy died, leaving me to fall in love with a man he left everything to. I'm so mad at him. I feel guilty for feeling anything but love for my father. But I do. I'm so pissed he died and stuck me with this asshole.

I grind my teeth remembering how I thought Liam practically stole that money from my father. All that anger comes back full force. He's a fucking liar!

I slowly turn my head as I hear the sound of the door

opening.

"Elle?" Liam asks with concern.

I ignore him and try to calm my racing heart. I watch from the corner of my eye as he walks towards the bed. I feel the bed dip as Liam sits next to me. Strong arms enclose me, but I push him away. "Don't fucking touch me!"

Liam looks struck by the venom in my voice. In my heart I feel a twinge of pain at the hurt look on his face. I'm mad I even feel that much. He doesn't deserve anything from me but scorn and suspicion.

They were trying to *kill* me. Because of him! He lied to me. How much has he lied? It hurts. Knowing he lied hurts so much. My chest feels like it's collapsing on itself. And what about daddy? I need to know right now. He better tell me everything. Like a slap to my face I realize he could just keep lying. And I'd have no way of knowing if he was telling the truth or not. I don't care though. I need to ask. I need to know what the hell is going on.

"Who were they?" I demand through my cries. After what I've been through, I deserve to know that much. "Who were those people?"

"You don't need to know their names," Liam says firmly, though I can hear the pain in his voice. "It won't change what happened."

I stare at him incredulously. I don't need to know their names? I almost got killed, and I don't need to know their names? What. The. Fuck. "You can't be serious!" I snap. "They tried to kill me because of you!"

Liam stares at me. "Yeah, and trust me, Elle, I'm going to make them fucking pay for it." He searches my grief-stricken face. I can tell he feels uncomfortable, but I don't give a fuck. He's the one that put me in this situation. "But you need to understand, sometimes in my line of business, things get violent. And I'm deeply sorry that you had to witness that today."

"Line of business?" I demand. "You're a restaurant owner!" I yell. "What kind of restaurant business gets in shootouts with thugs?"

"I'm a bookie," Liam corrects. My eyebrows shoot up in surprise. How many lies has he told me? My breathing comes in faster, and my blood heats with anger and betrayal.

"You're a fucking criminal!" I shout.

Liam swallows and clenches his jaw. I can tell I'm pissing him off. Good. He deserves it for all the shit he's put me through. "I'm not. What I do, it's not really illegal. There are some situations where I push the boundaries of the law... but it's still legal."

"You know what? Fuck you! You get me involved with all this shit, then you refuse to tell me what the hell is going on." I jump up from the bed and move out into the middle of the floor and start pacing. I don't even want to be near Liam right now. "I trusted you. I gave myself to you, even when I was telling myself that I shouldn't. Turns out, I was right. I shouldn't have given you a chance at all. You no good, lying bastard--"

"Elle. You need to--"

I stop pacing and gesture sharply. "How did you know my dad? Don't try to lie, or tell me I don't need to know." My voice dims, but I stare at Liam with all the rage I can manage. Just the mention of my father has the sadness creeping back in. But I can't let it show. I need to focus on my anger.

Liam holds my furious gaze for a moment, then sighs. "Fine," he says with firm conviction. "I'll tell you."

I hold in a sigh of relief. I'd expected Liam to tell me it was none of my business, just like he has been. "Go on," I command as though I have authority.

"Your dad didn't want me to tell you, but I think you deserve to know." He waits a moment and then breathes in deep. "Your dad needed money, bad," he begins. "He came to me to place a bet--"

"Bullshit!" I interrupt. I'm furiously shaking my head. Lies. More lies. "He wasn't a gambler--"

"Do you want me to tell you how we met or not?" Liam snaps. "I have no reason to lie to you."

We stare at each other. I don't know if I believe him or not. Regardless of what he tells me, I don't know if I'll believe him. "Are you going to listen to me?" he asks. There's a hint of condescension in his voice, and it pisses me off.

I glower and cross my arms over my chest, but reluctantly nod.

He waits to make sure I have my anger under control, and

then he tells me everything. About my father needing the money fast and not being able to sell the house. I listen as he tells me how my father came in and practically forced him to take 22 Wyoming. He tells me how they got close.

I don't know what to believe. I don't want to believe any of it. My head's spinning. He's a liar. That's all I can think. Daddy would never do that. He wouldn't go to a bookie. He couldn't have done something like that. Moreover, why would Liam have gone out of his way to help him?

I shake my head. "I have no reason to believe anything you say. It's all a bunch of lies."

"It's not. He was desperate for money, so I gave it to him."

"Why would you do that?" I ask him. I don't see why he would. He's just trying to make himself look better. He's lying to me again.

"'Cause he reminded me of my own father." I stare at him wordlessly, not believing what he's saying. My armor cracks a bit as I realize I don't know anything about Liam's father. I didn't even know he was dead. He only ever talks about his brother, Zac.

After a moment, Liam adds, "He died when I was younger." My heart sinks and feels heavy. A sadness passes his eyes, and I want to go and comfort him. But I don't know what to believe. I heave in a deep breath. My fingers itch to grab his hand and squeeze. I clasp them together instead. Even though I hurt for him, I can't forget that I have a fucking hitman after me because of him.

"I'm sorry," I manage to say. "About your father. I'm sorry." I wipe under my eyes and shake my head. I look him in the eyes and calm my breathing. "But I don't trust you. And I wish I'd never met you."

Liam goes still. He looks... emotionless. Like he's hiding everything from me. I feel sick. It's not true. What I said isn't true and I want to take it all back. At the same time, he hurt me. And I just hurt him back. I feel like such a fucking bitch. I hold my breath, scared of what he might say next.

But he says nothing, Liam walks out of the room not saying a word. I hear the sound of the door clicking shut and I finally breathe out slowly.

I'm left in silence. Silence so heavy it feels like I'm being suffocated. I clench my fists, wanting to scream at Liam. At the same time, I wish he'd come back so I could hold him and he could hold me. This is so fucked.

I wanna know if it's all true. If he really gave daddy that money to try to save his life. A sob leaves me unexpectedly, and I cover my face with both hands. Did he really do that for him? I take in a ragged breath. I don't know what to believe.

It all feels wrong, and my head is spinning with disbelief.

I wish I could just leave and pretend like this is all fake.

As though I don't love him. I never did.

But as I walk over and lie across the bed and begin bawling my eyes out, deep down in my heart, I know that's a lie.

I love this man. But I don't know if I believe him.

Chapter 23

Liam

It's late and I don't want to leave Elle, but at least one of these fuckers needs to die tonight. And the one I pick is Stephen. The fucker who tried to kill my girl and ruined everything I had with her. His life is over.

Zac's got his home address. Tyler said his wife's there. If she's there, he's gotta be there at some point.

I have to calm myself down, but I'm struggling. I've been on a knife's edge ever since she said those words to me.

I pick up my phone and swallow the lump in my throat. I'll make this right and that starts with killing these fuckers. I've got my gloves; I've got the wire. It's a silent easy kill. I know what to do. My uncle taught me. Tyler's father. When we went to live with him, I learned how to deal with shit the way the mob deals with it.

I shove the gloves and the wire into a small black bag and call my brother. It only rings once.

"You almost here?" I ask him without waiting for a hello.

"Just pulling in now." Perfect fucking timing. I walk to the foyer and look up the stairs. She's in my bedroom up there, and she's pissed. She deserves to be. But she's going to have to get over it. The doorknob turns and Zac pushes the door open. My brother's silent as he walks in.

"Just stay here and watch her while I go take care of this."

He nods his head. "I know. I've got my phone on me." I look up the stairs one last time and he follows my line of sight.

"She's still pissed?" I don't answer him. I told him what happened; he should know she's pissed. I'd be pissed. My lips are pressed into a straight line. My body heats with anger. This is how she's introduced to the only family I have.

It's fucked up. It's all fucked up, and it's all my fault.

"Tyler's on his way too." I give my brother a nod. I know he is. I almost had both of them stay here with her, but I can't be stupid about this and I need someone with me.

"I'll be back as soon as I can."

My brother's hand falls hard on my shoulder as I open the door wider to leave. I look back at him. "Make it quick and easy," he says.

I keep his gaze and nod. I'd like to draw it out. I'd like

to make him suffer. But I need to get back here. I don't like leaving her. Not until both of those assholes are dead.

Ian Dracho and his lackey are fucking dead. Then I can make it up to Elle. She'll forgive me. My heart lurches in my chest as I walk out into the cold. She has to forgive me. She has to.

I nod at Tyler as I make my way down to the end of the street. He's in his car and on the lookout in case anything happens or anyone sees what's going on. He could've done this, but I wanted to do it. I want to be the one to put an end to his life.

I sneak through the night, walking a few houses down and hide in the bushes at the back of the house, walking along the brick building. According to Tyler, he comes in this way. He parks in the garage and slips in the back. Like a fucking rat. He's afraid to come in the front door. He should be. He should be fucking terrified.

I peek in the small window above the kitchen sink and see a television on in the living room. I can't hear it, but I can see the back of a woman's head and the edge of the screen. She shouldn't be bothered. He won't see it coming; he won't even have a chance to scream. I resume my position in the cold night and stand behind the bushes next to the door. I'm completely still, dressed entirely in black. My thick leather gloves are on and the wire is wrapped tight over both hands. There's a good seven inches of slack. Enough to go around his throat.

My heartbeat picks up as I see him park his car. The lights shine on the door to the garage before it slowly opens. I can faintly hear the bass beats to whatever song he's listening too.

Time passes slowly and my heart beats even slower as his car disappears into the garage. I have to wait. Tick. Tick. Tick. Time goes slow. So fucking slow. I have to rein in my anger. I have to wait until he's here. So I can choke the fucking life out of the man who shot at Elle. He tried to kill her.

The longer I wait, the angrier I get, the tighter the wire is on my fingers. Finally, I hear a faint beep of the car's alarm. The side door opens and he starts walking along the pavers to get to the back door of his home. The night air is cold and I use it to calm myself. His keys jingle as he reaches for the right one to unlock the door. His head's down. He's not looking. It's fucking perfect.

I jump out and reach my arms up and over his head. His keys fall to the ground with a loud clink, and he tries to scream. But he barely gets any sound out as I pull the wire tight around his neck.

He could've killed her. It's all I think as I pull the wire tighter. My lungs stop working and my muscles scream in agony as I fight against this fucker. He *wanted* to kill her.

I pull the wire harder with everything in me. The thin wire digs into the gloves and feels like it's going to cut my skin, but I know it's not. I lift up as high as I can as he tears at his own flesh, desperate to pry the wire away. He tries to elbow me, tries to kick his leg back. He flails in my grasp, desperate for any escape. Any weakness. But I'm merciless in my pursuit of his death.

I take every hit and respond by pulling the wire tighter. The only sounds are crickets chirping and him struggling to breathe. Finally, he stops moving. I hold still for a long moment, unable to let go.

When I finally do, his body falls to the ground with a dull thud. His lifeless eyes are bloodshot and there are deep cuts on the sides of his throat from the wire.

I stare at him a moment, waiting for any signs of life as my breathing steadies. My head whips to the side and my heartbeat picks up as I hear the clanking of dishes in the kitchen inside. His wife is only a few feet away. She's going to end up finding this fucker out here. A part of me feels sorry for her. The rest of me doesn't give a shit.

I look back down at him and there's only one thing on my mind.

One down. One to go.

Chapter 24

Lizzie

I'm going to make Liam pay for this.

Last night, he left me alone. I heard him come in the house. I heard the two of them talking, but Liam never came up. Zac's the one who asked me to come down for dinner. I don't even know him. I don't know what to say to him. At one point, I would've been both excited and nervous to meet him. I would've wanted to make a good impression. But not now. I don't trust him either. I didn't eat and I didn't leave the room. I passed out eventually and for the first time in weeks, I woke up alone. I fucking hated it. I hated how I missed him.

He came up once today, and I ignored him. I'm not ready to talk about this. Not that he tried to say anything to me either. It hurt. But I guess that's what I get. And the moment I came downstairs, he left. He announced he was going to go *handle things.* My body chills at the thought of what he's doing. I can't take this shit. But I can't leave.

Liam has instructed his younger brother Zac to watch over me as if I'm some two-year-old. He said it's for my safety, but it's only annoying me. He's keeping me prisoner. That's what he's doing. I think what bothers me the most is the fact I wouldn't even be in danger if Liam had just been truthful from the beginning.

Like, if he cared so much about my safety, why did he get involved with me, knowing that he was mixed up in criminal activity?

Because he's a selfish bastard that only cares about himself, I tell myself. It hurts to think that though. I rock my leg back and forth; my heel hits the sofa. *Because he loves me* is the answer I want to believe. But that only makes me hate myself.

Lounging in the recliner, Zac stares back at me and then shakes his head. "You shouldn't be so pissed off. This is for your own good."

I roll my eyes. *You probably wouldn't know good if it hit you in the balls,* I think angrily. But I don't bother saying it. "Don't tell me how I should feel!" I hiss. "Do you know what happened to me? I almost got killed... all because of your dirtbag brother."

"Liam's not a dirtbag," Zac protests.

"Oh really? What about a piece of shit then?" I don't know why I'm acting this way. I don't really mean these things I'm saying. I'm just angry beyond belief.

Zac stares at the scowl on my face and then sighs. "Thanks, Liam, for pairing me with this diva."

"Oh fuck off," I snap.

"You're the one with the attitude."

"You're damn right. You spend a minute in my shoes and see if you don't have one after two seconds."

Zac goes silent and stares at me thoughtfully.

"Mind if I put the game on?" Zac asks after a long silence. He's obviously trying to change the subject. For all the good it'll do him, which isn't much.

I shrug. "Do whatever. I don't care. I just wanna leave."

Zac grabs the remote and flicks the TV on, turning it to a football game. "That wouldn't be a good idea. Liam doesn't want you to go anywhere."

I give him a withering look. "He has no right to keep me here... and neither do you!" Fed up, I stand up, intent on leaving.

Zac jumps up and gets in my way. "Where do you think you're going?"

I place my hands on my hips and command, "Get the fuck out of my way."

Zac shakes his head, eyeing me wearily. He's obviously as tired of this as I am. "I can't let you leave, Elle. Sorry." I'm struck by him calling me Elle. I don't like it. That's what Liam calls me. Not him.

"Lizzie," I correct him.

His brow furrows, but then he nods and says, "Lizzie, you need to sit your ass down."

For a moment, I debate on whether to make a run for it, then decide against it. There's no way I'm slipping past him.

I drop my hands to my sides in resignation. "Why are you doing this to me? You don't have to do this on your brother's behalf. I have every right to leave. You're committing a crime by keeping me here."

Zac keeps his eyes on me as if he's expecting me to pull a fast one. "Because you mean something to Liam, and he doesn't want you dead. And as far as committing a crime is concerned, I'd rather commit one than have to explain to my brother that I let you leave."

I scowl. "It's Liam's fucking fault I'm in danger. Not mine."

Zac sighs. "I know he's disappointed you by not being upfront about his business. But Liam is a good man, believe it or not. Dude's got a heart of gold. This is just something that comes with the territory in our line of work."

I snort and let out a wild laugh. "A good man? He's a liar!"

"I'm sure whatever he lied about wasn't to hurt you," Zac tries to reassure me. "Trust me. Liam isn't that type of person."

"The fuck he isn't," I mutter angrily.

Zac ignores me and I see little reason to continue arguing with him about Liam. After all, he's Liam's brother and sees him in a whole different light than I do. Of course he's going to be on Liam's side.

"I need to go to the bathroom," I say suddenly. "I've been holding it for a while."

Zac eyes me with suspicion for a moment. "Alright," he concedes.

I turn and begin walking toward the bathroom, but Zac follows me, practically breathing down my neck.

I turn on him and scowl angrily. "Can a girl use the bathroom without you breathing fire down my neck? Damn."

Zac looks like he's going to refuse, but then he bites his lower lip and says, "You have two minutes."

I walk into the bathroom and slam the door. Then I look around, searching for an escape. *Now how am I going to get out of here?* There's a window above the sink, but it looks like it's too small to get my whole body through.

I sit on the toilet and think. I don't even get a second before Zac's banging on the door.

"Give me a fucking minute!" I yell.

Zac's muffled response comes through the door. "Hurry up!"

Shit. Shit. Shit. I'm looking, but there's no way out. Unless I can drop ninety pounds in two minutes, I won't be getting out of that window.

"You've got ten seconds to come out of there, or I'm coming in."

Fucking A.

He quickly counts to ten and I don't budge.

"I'm not leaving, so you might as well come out," he growls.

I look around. There's no way out of here. I'm just wasting my time. Letting out a resigned sigh, I get up from the toilet and open the door.

"Feel better now?" Zac asks.

"Fuck off," I say. I brush past him, walk back over to the couch and flop down on it. I cross my arms over my chest and scowl. I'm so fucking pissed off. Why did this shit have to happen to me?

Zac walks over and sits back down in the recliner. He doesn't seem bothered by my nasty attitude in the least, and after studying me for a moment, he resumes watching the football game.

I sit there for about ten minutes, getting madder and madder, until I can take no more. "I'm just going to sleep," I announce, getting up.

Zac doesn't really react. I guess he's had it with my bitchiness. "Fine."

He gets up from his seat and escorts me to my room. I walk inside and am about to close the door when Zac says, "I know you're pissed off and all. And I really can't blame you. I think I would be too if I were in your position. But Liam really cares about you."

I roll my eyes. "Right. You were just calling me a diva.

Now you're agreeing with me."

"Seriously," Zac says, ignoring my rudeness. "He wouldn't be doing all this if you didn't mean anything to him."

I have no response. As much as I want to deny Zac's words, a small part of me wants to believe it's true. A small part of me wants to just give up the resistance and give Liam a chance.

It makes my heart hurt. It would be easy to fall back into his arms.

But I can't, I say to myself. *He's involved in crime... and I can't be with a criminal. He's dangerous.*

I stand there while Zac watches a range of emotions play across my face. He seems to be trying to reach out to me. Too bad I'm too angry and closed off to care. Or at least I'm doing a damn good job at pretending to be. I don't even know what's true anymore.

"Goodnight," Zac finally says softly. He can tell I'm preoccupied with my thoughts and conversation with me is all but useless. "Everything will turn out fine in the end. You'll see."

He gives me a moment to respond, but when I don't, he turns to leave.

Absently, I watch him walk off. And then I slowly shut the door. I look around the room, hellbent on finding a way out of here.

Chapter 25

Lizzie

God, I hope I don't fall and break my neck.

I peer out of the second story window of the bedroom. I've spent an hour debating on whether or not I want to do this. And I've decided that I do. It's a long way down to the sidewalk. But if I want to escape, I'm going to have to take my chances. Bad thing is, there's no real way down I can see other than jumping. I've been eyeing the gutters. I think they can hold my weight, and I can try to climb down.

Taking a deep breath, I climb out of the window, one leg at a time. It's so fucking cold. Outside, I hang on to the side of the window while I look for a way down. I can barely breathe. This is insane. It's fucking crazy, but I need to get away from this mess. I know I can't go home, but I can't stay here.

Holding my breath, I shimmy over to the gutter and grab hold. My fingertips hang on for dear life. My heart races and the chill in the air is actively working against me as it numbs my body. I breathe in deep and scoot over just a few inches, terrified that once I put my full weight on the gutter, it'll snap off. But it holds me. I finally breathe out, but only for a second before looking down. I close my eyes tighter. That was a mistake. It's a few more minutes before I can gather the courage to move in the slightest.

I prep myself to descend when I lose my footing. Shit! I gasp as I come close to plummeting to the ground. Luckily, I have a firm enough hold on the pipe that I save myself. I grip onto the gutter tighter than I have anything else in my entire life. Holy fuck, my heart is slamming in my chest and a cold sweat breaks out over my skin. This was so stupid. I wish I could take it back. I look up and think for a second about going back in there. But then I'm sentencing myself to be a prisoner. And I will not let that happen.

After a moment of deep breathing, I slowly restart my descent down. One inch at a time. That's all I need. I can barely breathe, but I keep moving down. By the time I reach the bottom, my arms are sore and my shoulders are throbbing. But I made it. And that's all that matters. I stand on shaky legs and look up. I can't believe I just did that.

I step away from the pipe and I look at the house, still

feeling slightly sick to my stomach. Through the window I can see the foyer and the stairs. The living room is on the other side of the house, so there's no way Zac could see I've escaped. I'm sure he's watching TV with the football game on and Zac reclining in the chair, his eyes glued to the screen.

Take that, Zac! I shout in my mind.

I wonder what Liam is going to say to his brother when he finds out that I escaped under his watch. Fuck, that's not going to be pretty. A feeling of guilt starts to settle low in my stomach. But I shake it off. I shouldn't feel guilty. The danger Liam put me in is unforgivable. I have to repeat that over and over in my head as if I'm trying to convince myself.

I turn away and start walking down the street. There are woods straight ahead. I just need to sneak in there and then I can figure out a plan. I know it'd be stupid to just walk out of the neighborhood. Liam could come home any minute and see me, and then all of this would be a waste.

I can't let him catch me. As I make it up the block, I take out my cell phone. I begin to dial the police, but then stop.

Obviously, those thugs need to go to jail, but if I call the police, there's a real possibility that Liam might, too. He will. Fuck! I know he will. I don't know why this bothers me. Liam's a criminal. He should go to jail. But I can't stomach the thought. I may not be able to stay with him, but I don't want anything bad for him. I don't want to hurt him or get him into trouble. I can't go home though. I'm not safe, and I'm on my own. I'm going to have to call the police. What choice do I have?

I'm vaguely aware of a white car driving toward me. I look up with my heart hammering in my chest, but with a brief glance, I see it's not Liam. I try to stay calm and just keep walking. The woods are past a few houses. I just need to get past them and then I'll be safe. The slam of a door pierces my consciousness and I jump with surprise, dropping my phone. It hits the ground with a loud smack.

I turn around and the car's parked in the middle of the street. I can't tear my eyes away from the man behind me. He's got his eyes pinned on me as he walks away from his car. My heart hammers in my chest and I know something's wrong. His eyes are so dark, nearly black, and the way he's looking at me sends chills down my body. I don't even try to pick up my phone as he takes a single step toward me. I take off running.

I hear him curse under his breath and then the thudding stomps of him chasing me. My eyes widen with shock. Holy fuck! He's coming for me. My mind races with ideas of who this man could be. He could be Liam's guy, parked out here to make sure I didn't get away. But he looks... cruel. He could be the man who shot at us. I want to scream, but my voice won't work. Fear cripples me, but I'm able to run. I can't stop running. Tears stream down my face from the sheer chill of the air battering my eyes as I run. I pump my arms and force myself to run as fast as I can.

My heart jumps up my throat and I bolt to the closest

house. My limbs scream with pain as I do everything I can to get away.

Without waiting to see if he's going to stop, I take off into the closest backyard, my heart pounding in my chest like a battering ram. I run faster than I ever have in my life. I can hear him still behind me, but I think I'm gaining ground. His breath is ragged. My own breath is coming in harsh pants. It hurts like a bitch to breathe in the cold air. But I ignore it all, darting into the woods.

I run straight through thin branches that whip across my body like lashings. I don't care though. I keep running through the pain.

After a few more minutes of all-out sprinting, I stop in a copse of trees to catch my breath and look around quickly. I don't see him. I listen for any noise, but I can't hear a thing. I focus on being as quiet as possible and listening. My back is to the tree and I'm too terrified to peek around it. Minutes pass. I don't know how many, before I take a look. No one's here. He's gone.

I sigh with slight relief, although I'm still trembling with fear and my heart is beating mercilessly against my chest. And then I remember. I dropped my phone. Shit. I have nothing. Fuck! I can't go back home, I don't have a car, I don't have my phone. I check my back pocket where I shoved my credit cards and ID. At least I have those still. They're hanging out of my pocket though. I check and see I still have them all as my breathing calms down. I lean my back against the tree again, this time for support rather than to hide behind it.

I look back again with paranoia, but no one's there. He was coming for us. No, he could be someone Liam knows or hired. I want to believe that. But I don't think it's true. My mind runs wild with all the possibilities of who he is and what he wants. I don't know, but the idea that he's going to kill one of them makes me want to run back there and warn Zac. Fuck! I can't even call Liam to warn him.

Shit, I don't know what to do. I feel so confused and hopeless. I shake my head and swallow the lump in my throat. I can't go back there. Even if I wanted to. What if he's there waiting for me?

This is Liam's life, and it's a dangerous one. I can't be a part of this. That man is the nail in the coffin. My heart clenches in my chest, but I refuse to give that pain any more attention. I take one more last look over my shoulder and then cautiously move through the woods. I just need to find an ATM, I'm not stupid enough to use my credit cards, I know that can be tracked. And once I have the little bit of cash in my bank account then I can find somewhere to stay. I can't go back to Liam and I can't go anywhere he could find me. I wish I could go to Nat, but that would only bring trouble to her doorstep. I can't do that to her.

I need to find a hiding place where I can think about what my options are. Although I feel like I don't have a single fucking option, other than calling the police.

Chapter 26

Liam

I know something's wrong the second I walk into the house. I close the door and look up the stairs.

Zac runs down them and his face falls as he slows down and sees it's me that's walked through the door. He's holding onto the railing like it's the only thing keeping him upright.

"What's wrong?" I ask him. He doesn't answer, he just looks at me and then the door. "Zac!" I yell his name to get his eyes on me. "What the fuck is wrong?"

He swallows visibly. "I just went to check on her." My body tenses as he pauses but then continues nervously, "Her window's open."

"She left?" I ask him. I'm surprised by how even my voice

is. Inside I feel like a caged animal only barely contained ready to destroy anything it can. But on the surface, I'm still and in control.

"She's," he pauses and takes in an unsteady breath as he registers my anger, "she's gone."

I'm so fucking pissed that he let her go. I storm off into the next room. I can't deny part of that anger is at her. She's putting herself in danger. It's also a mix of other emotions. *She left me.* My body tenses and the need to take it out on something is strong. Zac is looking like a good fucking option, but I keep my distance so I don't beat the shit out of him. I'll find her ass and drag her back here kicking and screaming if I have to.

I reach for my phone to call her and snort when I see her number calling me. I'm gonna lay into her. She can't fucking run off. She might be mad at me and that's fine if she wants to hate me for a little while, but she's staying with me, whether she likes it or not.

"Where are you?" I get right to the point as soon as I answer.

"I got a call about Stephen this morning. Message received, Liam?" I recognize Ian's voice immediately. Chills prick over my skin. It was her number. My heart beats rapidly, thudding against my chest plate. I know I saw her name.

"Ian," I answer simply, keeping my voice even as a cold sweat breaks out along every inch of my skin.

"We've got your girl here," he says confidently. My heart stops and I lean against the wall as my legs give out. No, not Elle. I swallow the thick lump that's growing in my throat and trying to suffocate me.

"I wanna hear her," I push the words out. Zac comes into the room and gives me a confused look. I feel sick to my stomach. I can't look at him. This can't be true.

"Sorry, but I can't; her mouth's full right now," he says and gives a disgusting laugh. I pound my fist against the wall in anger. Rage and adrenaline course through my blood. "How's this, we'll send a finger every hour until you fucks pay me the money you stole from me and shut down your business."

"Don't you fucking touch her!" Zac's face goes white as he takes in what's going on. I'm so fucking angry, my body's shaking.

"Come to Thirty-Five Lakeview," he says, and I try to hold in my rage so I can hear what he's saying. I know the place well; it's where they do their meets. "No weapons. We'll do a trade. You for her."

I can't hear a damn thing after the click, it's all white noise.

I look down at my cell again, it was definitely her number. They got her. They have my girl. I try to breathe, but it's hard. All at once, I snap out of it and the only thing on my mind is that I know I need to save her. I have to go to her. I have no other choice.

"Where's Tyler?" I barely recognize my own voice. Both of us were out looking for that asshole this morning. After

Stephen showing up dead and Ian being left all on his own, I figured he would be planning his leave. I was wrong. I was so fucking wrong. And it cost me the one thing I care about. I can hardly breathe.

"He's still upstate." Fuck! I grip my head in my hands. He's hours away, searching out Dracho's family homes. He's fucking useless to me now. I don't have time to wait for him to drive back down here.

"I'm sorry, Liam," Zac says but he can't even look me in the eyes. He tries to and his voice cracks as he continues, "I didn't--"

"It's not your fault." My blood won't heat. My lungs won't work. My body's failing me. He has her. I can't let him hurt her. Before I can even think about what I'm doing, my body's moving.

"Don't go, Liam! It's obviously a setup." Zac's talking, but I brush past him and keep moving. "He hasn't showed proof of life; she could already be dead. You think he's going to leave witnesses?" Zac grabs my arm and tries to hold me back. But I rip it out of his grasp and move quickly to the front door.

I don't even listen to his words. I don't care if he's right. They have her. They have my girl. I won't let them touch her. I won't let her die for my sins.

Zac's screaming at me, trying to talk sense into me. But I don't even register a single word coming out of his mouth. He grabs my chest, wrapping his arms around me to keep me back. He's smaller than me though. There's no way he can stop me.

"You can't keep me from her, Zac." I'll trade my life for

hers; it's done.

I snatch my keys off the front entry table and turn around, punching my brother square in the jaw. It's hard enough that he's knocked to the ground as his head slams against the floor.

He slowly comes to and cups his chin in his hand on the floor. He starts to get up, reaching for me. He's gonna do everything he can to keep me from going.

I take off before he gets up. I slam my car door shut as he comes barreling out the house, screaming for me to stop.

As the tires squeal and the car propels me forward, I see my brother racing to get to me in my rearview, screaming not to go. Screaming that he's sorry.

I drive faster than he can run and ignore the pain in my chest of leaving him this way.

I hate that I drove off without saying goodbye, but he'd never let me leave. I hate that he blames himself. He may always carry this with him. It's not his fault though. I don't blame him. All of this is my fault. I have to go to her. I have to save her.

Chapter 27

Lizzie

What do I do?

I'm sitting in my new hiding place, a rat-infested Motel 6 in a rundown part of town, wondering how to plan my next move. For the past thirty minutes I've been mulling over whether I should call the cops or not. It should be an easy thing to do, but my feelings for Liam are getting in the way.

There's gotta be a way to get rid of these guys without involving Liam, I think. But I can't think of any. I need to look out for me. I'm the one person I need to worry about. I can't stay here. I can't hide forever. But damn it, every time I press the buttons into the phone I feel like I'm literally stabbing Liam in the back. It's bad enough that I left him.

If only I didn't care about him. Then it would all be so easy. I'd dial up 911 without even thinking.

Maybe I should call him, I think to myself, *tell him it's over and explain that I have to call the police. I need protection, and I don't want it from him.*

I pick up the hotel's landline and dial Liam's cell. It rings for several seconds and then his voicemail picks up.

You've reached Liam. I'm busy right now, but if you leave your name and message I'll get back to you as soon as possible. Beep.

I sit there with the phone pressed to my ear for a moment and then hang up. God. Just hearing his deep voice again makes me feel weak. After a moment, I decide to try his house phone.

I get his voicemail again. When the beep comes, I've summoned the courage for a message.

"Liam," I say heavily over the huge lump in my throat. "I'm sorry. I didn't want to leave, but I just can't deal with what's going on. I can't be with... someone like you." I feel like a bitch for saying that. I close my eyes and hate myself. "I'm so sorry, Liam," I sob. "I really did love you, but this shit you're involved in... I can't. Goodbye." Feeling like my heart is going to burst, I hang up the phone.

I'm about to break down when the phone rings. I stare at it, wondering what I should do. It has to be Liam calling back. I'm conflicted about answering it. I'm supposed to be breaking it off with him and figuring out how to keep myself safe, not making it harder.

Screw it. I have to hear him out. I can already feel myself crawling back to him.

Taking a deep breath, I snatch up the phone. "Hello?" I say as my voice wavers.

"Lizzie!" My heart drops into my stomach. It's Zac.

"What do you want, Zac?" I ask flatly, pushing all the conflicting emotions away.

"Lizzie, are you alright?" Zac asks concernedly. I'm surprised by the worry in his voice. Apparently he's not pissed about me escaping right under his nose. "They don't have you, do they? Liam's going there now." His voice rises, "It's a setup; they're going to kill him."

Fear cripples me and my body chills. "What the hell are you talking about?"

My heart skips a beat. What the hell is going on? Liam's in danger? My body inches forward on its own. I grip the cord in my hand and wait with bated breath. "Where is he?" I cry, panicking. I rise from the bed as anxiety runs through me.

Zac quickly tells me what's happened, and I feel absolutely sick to my stomach. I listen to him anxiously until he's finished.

"We have to the call the police." I should've called already. If I'd called them, maybe this wouldn't be happening. This is all my fault. I never should've left. I cover my mouth with my hand, feeling like I'm going to throw up. If I hadn't left, he wouldn't be driving to his execution right now.

"No! Lizzie, don't--" Zac sounds frantic. I feel overwhelmed with heat and anxiety and not knowing what I should do, but knowing I need to do something. And I need to do it fast.

I'm about to hang up on Zac and call the cops when I realize that Liam's location is close by. Only a few blocks away. "I'll get to him; I'll stop him," I say as I begin to hang up the phone.

"Lizzie?" Zac sounds panicked. "Lizzie, what are you doing? Lizzie I need you to stay put--"

I hang up the phone, my mind and heart racing, and run my fingers through my hair. I'm shaking. My entire body is laced with anxiety.

I can't let Liam die. He's so close, and he's in danger all because of me.

Really though, what can I do? I'm an unarmed woman who's frightened out of her mind. I would be of no use to Liam in a gunfight. I'd probably only end up getting myself killed. I don't even have a gun.

But I can't let Liam die for me. Not after all we've been through. I don't care about anything other than saving him. I have to do something. I love him. It would kill me if he died. I can't let it happen.

I quickly grab my coat and put it on as I walk as fast as possible to the lobby. I nearly trip on the stairs; my feet just won't move fast enough. I need a taxi or something. I don't know. I need help. He needs help!

I walk out into the parking lot, where the bitter cold smacks me in the face. I search the street for a taxi or a street sign at least so I know which way to run when I see a car idling. Someone left it there to warm up. The keys are right there. I bite down on my lip and silently send a prayer of thanks.

My heart sputters. I wait half a second before I commit the first crime in my entire life and hop into the driver's seat. I slam the door shut and hit the gas. I don't look in the rearview mirror, I just drive, tires squealing as I turn out of the parking lot and onto the snow-dusted road. The back tires slip, and my breath catches in my throat. I struggle to put on the seat belt and keep the car going at the same time.

I can't fucking get into an accident. I swallow thickly and try to calm down and think of a plan.

I need to go to him. I need to save him.

I can't let him die.

Chapter 28

Liam

My heart's pounding in my chest. But it's so slow. Everything is slow. It's like I'm seeing everything differently now.

Ian's a piece of shit and I know he wants me dead. I know there's a possibility that he's gonna kill me as soon as I get there. But if he's got my girl, I have to try to save her. I'm not positive that he'll let her go. But I have no other options. If I don't go, she's dead. And I can't let that happen.

I can't let her die because of me. I'll never forgive myself. I look at the gun in the passenger seat as I slow down at the red light. I'm almost there. Maybe ten minutes, just a few blocks away. I'm resisting the urge to drive over the curb and push the pedal to the floor. But I can't get on a cop's radar. If I get pulled over, or worse, taken in, she's dead.

My hands are sweaty and I have to rub them off on my jeans before gripping the steering wheel again. The gun is the only thing on my mind. If I go in there with it, they'll probably find it and take it from me. If I were them, I'd check me. I wanna be protected, in case he goes back on his word, but they may see it and kill her. He said no weapons.

I slowly push the pedal down and the car moves. I'm driving to my death. But it's for her. I have to. I breathe out deeply. If there's a way to save us both, I'll do it. But if not, I'll die for her. I'll happily give my life to keep her safe.

My phone starts buzzing in my pocket. I only look to see if it's Ian. It's not her number. My brother keeps calling, but I can't answer. I know he's not on board with this plan. He'll hate me for leaving him like this. He doesn't understand. But when he finds someone he loves, he'll get it. He'll forgive me one day. And he promised to take care of her, that's what matters. My heart shatters in my chest. My phone won't stop going off. It's vibrating on my lap, and this time when I look it's my brother, but calling from my landline at 22 Wyoming. I bet he's trying different numbers, and I can't blame him. He just wants to convince me not to go. But it's not happening.

"I'm sorry," I say to no one as the phone stops ringing. I'm only a few blocks away. My resolve is firm.

I loved her before I even met her. I can't let her die.

This was all meant to happen. I couldn't save my father or Richard, but I can save her.

It'll be the one good thing I've ever done with my life.

Chapter 29

Lizzie

I put the pedal to the metal, running red lights and turning right on left turns and doing all sorts of crazy shit on my way to intercept Liam. I'm risking being stopped by the police, but I don't give a damn. I can't let anything happen to Liam. I can't afford to lose another person I love.

If I don't get there fast enough, I think worriedly, *they'll kill him. Why else would they tell him they have me? He has to know it's a setup.*

My heart pounds as I speed around a right corner, and my mind races through gruesome scenarios. I'm scared of what I might find when I find Liam. Will they have already gotten to him?

If they do, it will be all my fault. Fuck, I can't stand the thought. I feel so sick. I should've just listened to him.

It's hard to keep myself together and drive at the same time, but I'm doing it. I'm barely holding on, but I am.

I reach an intersection close to where Liam's supposed to be going. I know I'm going the right way. I know what road Zac said, and I'm close. I'm so close.

I have to slam on my brakes and stop at a red light because there's too much traffic. The tires slip on the slick road, but I manage to maintain control and avoid a collision. I slam my fist on the dash, hating that I have to waste even a second. Then I look all around, making sure I'm not missing anything.

Suddenly, I see Liam's car speeding up from the side road. Liam! Hope rises in my chest. He's alive. He's right there! "Liam!" I scream out even though there's no way he could hear me. I bang on the horn, over and over. I lay all my weight on it. Staring at him. Begging him to look at me.

But he doesn't. Everyone around me is watching. They don't know. He's about to drive to his death, and I'm stuck watching him, unable to do anything about it. No! I honk again and again as he gets closer to the intersection. But he's not seeing me. He's not looking anywhere but straight ahead.

With how fast he's going I'm sure he won't see me. I can't let him pass.

With only seconds to react, I floor the gas pedal and smack into the car ahead of me. I push down hard, shoving the car out of my way as my own car jolts forward. I hear the screams and honking from the other drivers gathered at the red light. They're yelling and pissed, but I don't care. Faster! I have to go faster. He's so close. He's almost at the intersection in front of me. I slam on the gas and head out into the middle of the intersection just as Liam comes speeding through the center.

I know the meet is right there. If I don't do this, I won't be able to get to him in time. We're both going too fast. I speed my car ahead and close my eyes, knowing he's going to hit my car on the passenger side. But it's the only way I can stop him. I lay on the horn and speed my car right in front of his and I prepare my body for the blow.

The screech of metal and shattering glass is deafening as he broadsides me, spinning my car out of control. My body's forced to the right with a stinging pain from the seat belt. My head's violently whipped to the side as the car comes to a halt and I slam my head on the driver's window with a loud crack.

Fuck! That hurt. As the car comes to a sudden stop, I wince and slowly lift my hand to my head. I look down at my fingers and see blood.

My body aches all over, and there's a sharp, stabbing pain in my side. A pounding sensation throbs inside of my skull, causing black spots in front of my vision.

I feel like absolute shit.

"Liam," I call weakly. He's the only thing I care about. I'm so dizzy and can barely see anything, but I can't think about anything other than Liam.

"Liam," I repeat in a half-choke, half-cry. *Please don't be dead.* My heart beats faster as I try looking out my shattered windshield.

Groaning, I fumble with my seat belt, trying my best to undo it, but it's stuck. I have to get out of here. Now. But I feel so fucking weak.

For a moment I fear I'll get stuck in the car and get burned alive. In a panic, I start rattling my seat belt, hoping it will just loosen. It doesn't unsnap. Fuck.

Suddenly, my door is being ripped open and a deep, familiar voice asks, "Elle?" His voice is full of worry, but also disbelief.

Relief floods my body at the sight of Liam. He looks bruised and battered with a few cuts on his face and arms, but other than that, I've never seen him look so damned good in my life.

"Liam, don't go!" I yell at him, shaking my head.

"You're here," he says as he looks at me with utter disbelief before looking down at where I'm trying desperately to get the buckle undone. I need to get out of this fucking car and hold him. He's really okay.

Without hesitation, Liam bends into the car and rips my seat belt off. Then he pulls me out and into his arms. I hold on to him even though my body is screaming in pain. I just need to hold him.

He squeezes me gently. I feel like I can finally breathe. I grip on to him tighter, refusing to let go as he kisses me over and over again. "I'm so sorry," I whisper against his chest.

Liam hugs me close again. "Jesus, Elle." He pulls back to look at me. "Are you okay?"

I shake my head. "You were going to die." I hold him closer and just try to breathe. "You were going to die for me?" I pull back to look at him. His fingers gently touch the gash on my scalp.

Liam peers at me with disbelief. "I would do anything for you. I love you, Elle."

My eyes prick with tears at the admission. "I love you so much."

Hot tears begin streaming down my face like a waterfall and the words start gushing out. "Oh my God, I'm so sorry that I left you. I wasn't thinking. I was just so... so scared." The words tumble out of my mouth. I shake my head, wishing none of it were true. If I'd just listened to him, none of this would have happened.

Liam kisses me on the forehead, pulling me close. "It's okay. You're okay, that's all that matters."

I look up at him, my heart clenched tight, needing his forgiveness. I know this is all my fault. "Please forgive me."

Liam gently caresses my tearstained cheeks and shakes his head. "I can't forgive you, Elle." My breath catches in my throat, and I feel tears welling up again in my eyes. I've ruined things between us. It's too late.

"I can't forgive you, because you haven't done anything

wrong." He kisses me then, a deep, long lingering kiss that leaves me wanting for more. When he pulls away I'm breathless, and in pain. The car crash has banged me up pretty good.

"We need to go before the cops show up," he says urgently.

I look around, and people are stopped at street corners staring at us and taking pictures with their cell phones. Some are even on their phones, talking while surveying the devastation. Cars are starting to pile up as they try to maneuver past the wreck.

"Shit! Get down!" Liam suddenly yells, yanking me to the ground just as I was starting to stand, and pulling us close to the open driver's door. I get a quick glimpse and see the man from before, the man with the cold, dark eyes. My heart hammers in my chest. My body feels paralyzed.

The crack of gunfire splits the air and I let out a piercing scream as another whizzes by us and hits Liam's car behind me. Immediately, Liam pushes me against the car and covers me with his hard body, sandwiching me between hard metal and his protection. So many people are screaming and running. I close my eyes tightly as my heart leaps in my chest.

Oh my God, I think, frozen with terror. *We're going to die.* My fingers dig into him, holding on as tight as I can as my body tries to curl into a ball. The cold wind travels beneath the open door. We hardly have any cover.

Another gunshot fires off and I can't help that my body jolts with the loud bang of the bullets plastering the car. Liam continues to shield me and I wish I could protect him. I can't bear the thought of him being hit. Each second that passes seems like an eternity, but finally the gunfire ceases.

Liam immediately goes into action. He rolls off of me, staying crouched down.

"Get in your car and drive!" Liam orders, keeping his eyes focused ahead, looking for the target.

I hesitate, worrying about what's going to happen to him.

Liam gestures sharply, his face twisting in anger at my hesitation. "Go! I'll cover for you. You need to get out of here!"

"You can't stay here!" I protest just as three more gunshots go off. I wince and duck down out of instinct. My heart can't take this. I'm so fucking scared, I'm shaking.

Liam peeks over the hood of the car. "Don't worry about me. I'll be fine." When I don't budge, he reaches into his pocket and brings out his cell. He taps the screen, speed-dialing someone.

"Zac, where are you?" Liam asks. "Yeah. We're on South Street. Yeah. Bring heat." He takes the phone from his ear and looks at me. "I'm going to be fine. Zac's." He cups my face in his hands. "You don't have to worry about me."

I stare into his eyes and all I see there is love. I can't leave him. I won't! "Please, I can't do this right now," I croak. "I need you."

Liam shakes his head angrily. "Get in the car! Now."

"No!" I yell, shaking. "I'm not leaving without you." *If something happens to you, I won't be able to live with myself.*

"Fuck," Liam growls. He brings the phone back to his ear and says, "Zac, don't come. I'm leaving with Elle... Yeah, I have to get it. I'm not gonna leave without trying to take him out." He hangs up and pockets the phone.

"Stay here and don't move," he says sternly and quickly crouches down and goes to his car that's just behind mine.

"No!" I yell out and try to reach for him, but he's gone before I can get to him. He's completely unprotected for the briefest of moments, but I can't stand that he's putting himself in danger. I think about losing the cover of the door and trying to follow him, but I feel his body slam against the back of the car, before I can move.

He comes back with a gun and cocks it. "Get in."

I'm so fucking scared, but I do as he says. Keeping low, I climb in and crawl to the passenger seat. Another bullet hits the car and I stifle my scream.

"Keep your head down," Liam orders, starting the car while keeping his head low. As if in response to his order, several bullets come flying through the windshield, raining glass on my head.

I cry out, my heart beating so fast it feels like it's going to explode. Small shards of glass cover the seat and my body. I pull the sleeves of my sweater over my hands for protection. The sounds of sirens wail in the distance and I feel a moment of relief. The cops are coming.

"I won't let him live." Liam say, making my body chill. He

responds to the gunshots with a few shots of his own. *Bang*! *Bang*! *Bang*! I hear someone yell something, but I can't make out what it is. It's so quiet now. All I can hear is my own breathing. I steal a glance over at Liam; he looks so intense; he doesn't even look like he's breathing. I jump when he fires off two more shots. I hear a short cry and then nothing.

Liam finally sits up and looks behind us as he puts the car into reverse and hits the gas. We hit his car and then he puts the car in drive and takes off.

A few precious moments of silence pass as the car takes off. I'm still low and Liam's still tense. "Did you get him?" I finally ask, my heart still racing.

Liam looks at me, dropping the gun in his lap.

"Yeah," Liam replies, "I got him." He puts his hand down for me to grab, still keeping his eyes on the road. I slowly rise and look around as Liam pulls off into a neighborhood. "It was only him. It's done." My body eases slightly. "It's over." He says with finality.

I struggle to believe it's true and to know what to say. We drive in silence. *It's over*.

"We gotta ditch this car." He looks at me with sympathy in his eyes.

I can hardly breathe. This doesn't feel real.

"Hey," Liam says, holding my hand. "It's okay now."

It doesn't feel okay though. I'm still shaking.

The car slows a few blocks down, and Liam shuts down

the engine. He looks over at me, his jaw clenched. "Promise me." He pauses a moment to take in a deep breath. "Promise me that you'll never do something so stupid again." His voice is hard, cold, nothing like what I expect from the heated look in his eyes.

Tears pool in my eyes. He seemed okay when we were getting shot at, now he's acting like he's pissed at me. "I told you why I did--"

"You left me," he growls. "You left me when you knew you were in danger."

"But," I begin to protest, but I can't think of any words. I'm so overwhelmed, and I know at the time it had felt like the right thing to do.

"I don't want to hear it," he says sharply. "Tell me right now that you'll never do that again. Ever." I'm shocked by the anger in Liam's voice, and I stare at him with my mouth open. Then it slowly dawns on me; he's scared. He's so scared he was going to lose me. He's literally shaking.

He reaches across and strokes my injured face. "You don't know how much you mean to me, Elle," he tells me. "If something had happened to you..." His voice trails off, and on his face is a pained expression.

I swallow the lump that forms in my throat. "I'm sorry, Liam. I promise you. I'll never do that again."

He leans across the console and kisses me. I easily part my lips and kiss him back with the same passion he has for me.

He pulls away from me and looks into my eyes. My heart's racing, and everything feels like it's too much to handle.

"This--" Liam begins to say, as he must sense the worries I have. "This will never happen again. This isn't okay, and this isn't normal."

I search his eyes. "I've never lied to you, Elle." I part my lips to protest that bullshit, but he puts his finger up to my lips and continues, "I've kept the truth from you, but I've never lied. And I promise you this. I fucking love you, and I will never let anything like this happen again."

I don't know what to think, or what to say. All I know is what I feel. And right now all I feel for him is love. I don't trust it though. I feel stupid for even being with a man like him.

"I'm done with this shit. I'm completely done. All I want is you. I will do anything and everything to have you and to keep you safe." Something shifts inside of me. As if those were the words I was waiting for.

"Just stay with me." He says as his thumb brushes over my lips. "I'll always protect you, and I know with everything in me that I love you. Just stay with me and let me be there for you."

It's so easy to give in, and I want to. I lean into his hand and close my eyes as I nod my head. I can be with this man. I know it in my heart. He was going to die for me. If that's not true love, I don't know what is.

"I will." I open my eyes and see nothing but devotion in his. "I love you too, Liam."

Chapter 30

Liam

She's barely said a word since I've brought her back. I expected her to demand I take her back to her place, but instead she keeps looking over at me with worry in her eyes. Like she can't believe we're really safe.

"You still mad at me?" Zac asks her. The three of us are in my living room. I know the cops are going to show up at some point. They'll probably have a warrant too since my car was at the scene of the crime, and there's probably witnesses who saw me. It's alright though. My uncle's still got contacts, and I'm sure I'll get off without a hitch. Until they get here though, I'm going to be on edge.

"I'm not mad at you," Elle finally answers. Her voice is

small and lacking the bite she usually has. She hasn't eaten anything. I know she's still rattled from everything that happened. I wish I could take it all back.

"Then play some cards with me," Zac offers, holding up a deck. We were playing earlier to pass the time and help Elle get out of her funk. She's not used to this, but she doesn't ever need to get used to it. I swear I'll never let this kind of thing ever happen again.

Elle narrows her eyes at Zac before responding, "You're a filthy cheater." Zac laughs and I let out a chuckle, pulling her closer to me on the sofa.

"You're a poor loser," Zac says, setting the cards down on the table.

We've got the news on, but other than a little snippet earlier, there's nothing about what happened. Ian Dracho is dead. I already knew he was, but seeing it on the television made Elle relax somewhat. I shot that fucker right between his eyes and then his throat. I've never felt so much relief in my entire life. I remember how tense I was, waiting with slow and steady breaths. I just needed him to come up so I could take another shot. Although it was only seconds, the time passed so damn slow waiting for my target to show himself.

I shake off the tension creeping up on me and look down at Elle. I have to tell her everything. I promised her I would. I know she's not going to like it, because it's not pretty, but hopefully it'll earn her trust.

"You okay?" I ask Elle quietly as Zac gets up and leaves the room.

"I'm scared, Liam," she whispers back, and I kiss the tip of her nose and push the hair out of her face.

"There's no reason to be scared." I give her a small smile. "I know it's gonna take a little while before all that shit gets out of your system, but I swear to you, it's all over. Everything's okay."

She searches my face for something, and whatever it is, I hope she finds it. She settles into my lap and puts her cheek against my chest.

"You belong here, Elle." I kiss the top of her head. "You belong with me."

She huffs a small laugh and gives me the faintest of smiles. "Yeah, I do."

"You know I love you, right? And that I'm really sorry." I say the words with every ounce of sincerity I have. I hope she knows it's true. I can't do anything but keep telling her and showing her until she believes me.

"I know," she says as she leans up and plants a kiss on my lips. "I love you, too."

Two weeks later

Elle's finally coming around. At first she was hardly talking to me. But she wouldn't let go of me. She wouldn't let me out of her sight. Everything was cleared with the cops; I got off easy, no charges. My uncle came through with his connections. I told my brother and my cousin that I was out and they agreed it was for the best. Even after all that, she still looked at me like I was gonna be killed any second.

I'll earn her trust again. And to do that, I'm starting with this move. I'll live an honest life with her. I know she loves me and I love her, so the rest will come with time.

I'm moving in with her. Technically it's to a new place, but it was her choice, a place close to her school. Just for five months until she's done, then her ass is coming home. I may not be working with my family anymore, but I want to be by them. And so does she.

She wants to work in a school, so there's plenty of jobs for her when we move back here. And she wants to come back. Which makes me happy. She doesn't have any family, but I do and I don't want to leave them.

Not now.

I want as much family around us as we can get. And as soon as she's ready and trusts me again, I'm gonna do right by her and putting a ring on her finger. I don't care if this is fast and it's only been a couple of months. What we've been through is hard, but we did it together. I need her, and she needs me. That's all that matters.

I look around my bedroom and make sure I've got everything packed.

I do, everything's all set. Except for the letter. I've held onto it. But I haven't been able to give it to her. I take a deep breath and slip it out of the envelope. We're moving forward with our lives and I want her to see for herself what her old man was thinking. She should know.

I take deliberate steps to where Elle's standing in the kitchen.

"Hey Elle," I say and lean in to kiss her cheek. "You ready to read it?" I ask.

She looks at the note and a flash of sadness crosses her eyes as she registers what it is. She gives me a small nod. "You said he reminded you of your dad?" she asks as she walks toward me. The reminder makes my heart pang.

"Yeah, a little," I admit.

"I'm sorry." She cups my face in her hands and plants a kiss on my lips. "I'm sorry, Liam." She holds my gaze and I look back at her, not knowing what to say. It was so long ago, but it does hurt from time to time still. I kiss her on the lips and pull her closer to me. I just wanna hold her. That makes everything feel better. Having her to love makes the pain go away somehow.

I sit at the small table in the kitchen and wait for her to

take a seat on my lap. I kiss her cheek, but it doesn't help. She still gets a little sad whenever her old man comes up. I can't blame her. It's gonna take time.

Her hand rests on my shoulder and she leans in, resting her cheek against my chest.

I shake the letter out and hold it so she can easily read it, too. I know this is gonna be hard for her. But I'm here. We'll get through this together.

CHAPTER 31

LIZZIE

"I can't believe how well business is doing!" Nat cries as she sets out another fresh batch of her infamous sugar cookies.

Since it's the day before I leave, I figured I'd come spend time with Nat before I say goodbye. I feel like myself again, most of the time. When I'm with Nat, it's easier. She brings out the old me.

Only when I arrived, I found Nat swamped with customers. I offered to help Nat keep up with the demand. Unfortunately, it took just a few minutes of being bossed around before I wanted to strangle her.

Luckily for me, Nat's two new hires came in to help, April and Haley, and they're busy running the cash register and filling the orders, allowing us a moment to chat in the back and catch up on each other's lives.

"I can," I say, fighting back the urge to snatch one of the fresh cookies off the tray. They smell damn delicious and it's hard to keep my eyes off of them. Seriously, I could eat the entire batch by myself right now! Ever since making up with Liam, my appetite has returned in full force. I think I've put on a good ten pounds and even have my voluptuous figure back. "Have you tasted your cookies lately? They're out of this world amazing!"

Nat grins at me as she gently prods one of the cookies to test its softness. "You're such a suck-up, you know that?"

I wink at her. "Why wouldn't I be? After all, you're like the town's queen of baking."

Nat pokes another one of her cookies and snorts. "Goddess of baking is more like it. Hell, I should have my own show on the Food Network with all the work I put in."

I raise an eyebrow. "My my, modest, aren't we?"

Nat laughs. "I'm just playing. You know I don't have a big head like that."

I nod, my stomach growling. I can't stop eyeing those delicious cookies. A second longer, and I'm going to need handcuffs. "Mmmhmm. Sure. Anything you say. Just wait until you expand and open up your next bakery. Then you'll probably fall over from the weight of your head."

Nat laughs. Then she groans. "Ugh. Don't tell me about

it. I was already looking at my balance sheet the other day and realizing I'll have this paid off by the end of the year, which will give me room to expand if I want." She sighs. "I've already started stressing out, staking out prime locations for a new shop in the town over."

"Take it slow," I advise, still staring at those damn cookies. "Don't worry about that until it gets here. You have all the time in the world to enjoy the success you're having now." Screw it! I can't take it anymore. I take one of Nat's cookies and pop it in my mouth. The rich, delicious sweetness invades my taste buds, and my eyes roll back in my head at the taste. God, so good.

Nat glowers at my theft, but deep down I know she loves that I can't keep my hands off her cookies. It's the hallmark of a grandmaster baker. "You know what? You're right. Speaking of which, how are things with you and Liam?"

I pause, my heart fluttering in my chest at the thought of Liam. He's been the best lately, renting out the perfect place for us while I'm going to school, and doing what he can to make my life easier. It warms my heart, because it means he cares, and he's trying to make up for everything that went down. Still, I feel guilty about him paying for everything, but he insists not to worry about it. He says I'd do the same for him if I were in his position. And I would.

I can hardly contain the smile on my face as I finish off the delicious morsel. "They're good." *More than good.* I told

Nat about Liam the other day. A little more than I should have, I think. I even included Liam's dad dying, him staying with his uncle and how he's a bookie. I probably shouldn't have said anything about the business. But Liam keeps saying it's legal. And he's quitting. For me. That's the only reason I told her. I pop another delicious cookie in my mouth to keep in all the other details that have been dying to come out. She doesn't need to know about everything that happened. No one does. I want to forget it all and pretend like those few nights never existed.

Nat's eyes flash dangerously at my bold theft, and I hold in a laugh. "I don't know Liz, isn't this rather fast to be doing all this?" she asks, watching me gobble down the cookie. "After what happened, I'm kind of worried about you."

"Don't be," I say. "I know it's only been two months, but Liam and I... We've really gotten to know each other." It's hard to put into words what I feel. I feel like he's my soul mate. Nat would have to find her own to understand.

Nat doesn't look totally reassured as she says, "I hope so."

Then she asks, "But what's he going to do while you're at school?"

"A lot!" I say excitedly, momentarily forgetting the tray of cookies. I've been dying to tell her of Liam's plans to build up his investments.

"Well, he's got enough cash flow to invest in a few companies." He told me he loved the restaurant, but he didn't want another. Something about numbers and return on investments. I didn't quite keep up with what he was saying, but he was excited to tell me about the other companies.

Nat makes a surprised face when I'm done. "That's odd."

"What?" I ask.

"With how hot Liam is, I'd thought he'd have shit for brains. This guy sounds smart as hell."

"That's not nice," I protest. She shrugs.

"Sorry. But it's the truth. Guy like him could make millions on his looks alone, instead he chooses to use his brain. I know if I could model and make megabucks, I sure in the hell wouldn't be breaking my back doing this." Nat shakes her head sorrowfully.

I chuckle. "He totally looks like he'd be some vapid model instead of head of his own empire--"

Nat suddenly motions with her hands as if to warn me to shut up. "Speak of the devil."

Strong arms enclose me, and a deep voice murmurs in my ear, "Speaking of what devil?"

My heart does several backflips. "Liam!"

I turn in his arms to be greeted with a deep, smoldering kiss that has me wanting to strip naked and fuck right then and there in the back of Nat's bakery. In front of Nat.

We're both so lost in the kiss that it takes Nat to break us out of it.

"Get a room! Jesus!"

I pull away from Liam, my face burning. "Sorry!"

Nat is unconvinced. "I'm sure."

Liam chuckles, totally unashamed by our hot and heavy display of affection and wipes his lips. I'm sure I taste like sugar cookies, but Liam probably likes it. "Hey Nat."

Nat does a little wave. "Hey Liam. How's it hanging?"

Liam grins and I know he's thinking something dirty. "Alright. How's the bakery going?"

"Absolutely fantastic," she says, gesturing to the front of the shop. "Can't you tell by the line outside?"

Liam shakes his head. "I snuck in the back."

"Figures." Nat scowls at me. "I wonder who left the door open."

I look innocent. "Surely not me."

Nat scowls harder, threatening to send me off into gales of laughter.

Liam stares at Nat's fresh batch of cookies. "So are these the famous cookies I've been hearing so much about around town?"

"Yes they are," I'm quick to say. I gesture at the tray. "You should try one." *Heaven knows, I could eat five more.*

"I think he already has," Nat growls, staring pointedly at the five empty spots on the tray. "Sugar lips."

Liam laughs as he realizes why I tasted like a sugar cookie. "Well, if that's the case, I guess I have to have one. 'Cause Elle here tasted sweeter than usual." He walks over to the tray and looks at Nat for permission.

Nat waves him on. "Go ahead, you certainly can't do any more damage than your girlfriend did."

"I resent that," I say.

"Bite me."

"Don't tempt me."

Liam isn't paying attention to our bickering. He takes a cookie and pops it in his mouth. His eyes widen a moment later. "Shit. These are really good," he says.

Nat beams with pride. I can tell she takes his compliment to heart since he's someone that knows good food. "Thank you."

Liam shakes his head, grabbing another cookie. "No. Thank you. Seriously, I could totally see you going on TV and winning one of those baking contests and then ending up with your own reality show."

Natalie looks at me with an 'I told you so" look. "See, Lizzie? What'd I tell you?"

"Careful, Liam," I warn. "You give her too many compliments, her head might explode."

"Better than my stomach exploding from eating too many cookies," she retorts. I giggle at her insult.

"If you're looking for a business partner, I could certainly help you out in the investment." I'm surprised by Liam's offer and judging by the look on Nat's face, so is she.

"I'll..." she starts to say and then purses her lips. "I'll have to think about it," she says confidently and then nods with a smile. "But thank you. If I need a partner, I'll keep you in mind."

"Fair enough," Liam says with a smile. "You ready to go, Elle?" His eyes are hooded with lust as he looks at me, and a shiver of anticipation shoots up my spine.

"Yes," I say huskily. "Just let me say bye to Nat and then we can go."

He pulls me into a light kiss that makes me weak in the knees. "Don't keep me waiting long." He gives Nat a nod goodbye, and she does the same in return as he walks out the back door.

"I'm gonna miss you," I say with a pout.

She gives me a pout back and embraces me in a hug.

"We'll be back in a few months." We already talked about it. I wanna stay close to home, and he wants to be with his family. I have two semesters left and then we'll be moving back here.

"Bye Nat." I give her another embrace and turn to leave but stop to say, "Don't you ever stop baking."

Nat gives me a look. "Are you crazy? I'll never stop doing that. Who else is going to make your wedding cake?"

As we drive down the road, the orange glow of the sunset basks us in its radiance. We pass familiar places on the way out of town, and I'm almost overwhelmed by the feelings. I'm going to miss this place. Nat, the bakery, daddy's house. Everything. Even if it's only a few semesters. Thinking of the house makes tears prick in my eyes. I don't wanna leave. Emotions creep up on me out of nowhere. I've been doing so good lately.

Seeming to sense my sadness, Liam looks over at me just as we hit the highway. "It's going to be okay, Elle."

I smile at him and stroke his arm. "Thank you," I say simply.

"No, thank you. For sticking by me through all the bullshit I put you through."

I stare at him, love filling my heart until I feel like it's going to burst. He didn't have to thank me. I'd die for him at this point. I was so terrified of losing him. It was all I could think about. Now I realize there's no way I'm letting him go. No matter what happens.

"I love you, Liam," I breathe, meaning it with all my heart.

Liam looks over at me, his eyes filled with love. "I love you too, Elle."

Epilogue

Liam

TWO YEARS LATER

I can't stop looking at his little feet. He spreads his toes and squeals as Elle tries to latch him on again. They're so tiny. Everything about him is tiny. We took his little footprints and put them with the rest of the valuable things that are priceless to us. My father's silver pen, her father's note, and our little man's footprints. We've gotta find the perfect place to put them, but until then they're in my office, proudly on display within a shadowbox Elle bought just for them.

I look up at Elle and she looks so tired, but also worried. He's lost eight percent of his weight and I keep telling her it's normal. So do the doctors, but she's scared.

She takes in a steady breath and repositions our little man. I watch as he shakes his little head back and forth, and finally the squeals stop and I can faintly hear suckling.

Elle smiles slightly, and her body sags in relief. She's doing such a good job. She's so critical of herself, and she doesn't even realize what a wonderful mother she is already. Everyone from her work agrees. She's a counselor at the high school and she loves it there. I love that she has the entire summer off for our little one. Last year it was for our honeymoon. I look down and smile at the platinum band on my ring finger. After our big wedding, we took two months off to unwind. Planning that shit really stressed her out, but it was all worth it though. She was a beautiful bride, and now she's an even more beautiful wife and mother.

She doesn't have to work though. Not with all the investments we have. She wants to, and that's fine with me, as long as she's happy.

"He's perfect," I say just above a murmur. Her eyes meet mine and they shine with love.

"He looks like you," she says as she looks back down at our son, Michael Richard Axton. We named him after both of our fathers. "I think his eyes are going to stay blue, too."

He's not even a week old yet, but he's so loved.

I settle back on the new sofa. Elle didn't want to take any of the furniture from her stepfather's. It's all been donated. All except for his leather recliner. That's still in the house. It's mostly empty, and we have cleaners coming and a crew to fix it up some. But we aren't selling it. The house next door is being rented out, and her family home may be rented out too someday. But for now, it's for storage until Elle says otherwise. She needs time still. We both do. Losing someone you love is never easy. Grief is a journey. I don't think it ever really ends.

I take in a deep breath and look around our new place. We've still got boxes of things that need to be put away, and bottle nipples and pacifiers to sterilize. Our little man came five weeks early and gave us a scare. So the new place is a mess. Elle didn't even get a real baby shower.

Nat's throwing her a surprise one next week. She said it's more of a sip and see, whatever the hell that means. Either way, little man has been showered with love and so has Elle.

I can't even tell her how I feel. There are no words.

Little man sighs and pops off Elle's nipple. I look into her eyes and see a flash of worry until he settles against her breast and nuzzles down to go to sleep.

She sighs with content and gently pats his back.

I lean in to kiss her cheek, but she turns her head and takes my lips with hers. I smile against her lips and brush the tip of my nose against hers. My heart swells in my chest.

I say the only thing I know that's absolutely true, "I love you, Elle. I love you two so damn much."

She reaches her hand out to take mine and squeezes. "I love you too, Liam."

About the Authors

Thank you so much for reading our co-written novel. We hope you loved reading it as much as we loved writing it!

For more information on the books we have published, bonus scenes and more visit our websites.

More by Willow Winters
www.willowwinterswrites.com/books

More by Lauren Landish
www.laurenlandish.com

Made in the USA
Middletown, DE
06 March 2025